The Red Dragon

SELECTED FICTION WORKS BY L. RON HUBBARD

FANTASY
The Case of the Friendly Corpse
Death's Deputy
Fear
The Ghoul
The Indigestible Triton
Slaves of Sleep & The Masters of Sleep
Typewriter in the Sky
The Ultimate Adventure

SCIENCE FICTION
Battlefield Earth
The Conquest of Space
The End Is Not Yet
Final Blackout
The Kilkenny Cats
The Kingslayer
The Mission Earth Dekalogy*
Ole Doc Methuselah
To the Stars

ADVENTURE
The Hell Job series

WESTERN
Buckskin Brigades
Empty Saddles
Guns of Mark Jardine
Hot Lead Payoff

A full list of L. Ron Hubbard's
novellas and short stories is provided at the back.

*Dekalogy—a group of ten volumes

L. RON HUBBARD

The Red Dragon

GALAXY
PRESS

Published by
Galaxy Press, LLC
7051 Hollywood Boulevard, Suite 200
Hollywood, CA 90028

Printed in the United States of America.

ISBN-10 1-59212-328-7
ISBN-13 978-1-59212-328-5

Library of Congress Control Number: 2007903625

Contents

Stories from Pulp Fiction's Golden Age

A ND it *was* a golden age.
The 1930s and 1940s were a vibrant, seminal time for a gigantic audience of eager readers, probably the largest per capita audience of readers in American history. The magazine racks were chock-full of publications with ragged trims, garish cover art, cheap brown pulp paper, low cover prices—and the most excitement you could hold in your hands.

"Pulp" magazines, named for their rough-cut, pulpwood paper, were a vehicle for more amazing tales than Scheherazade could have told in a million and one nights. Set apart from higher-class "slick" magazines, printed on fancy glossy paper with quality artwork and superior production values, the pulps were for the "rest of us," adventure story after adventure story for people who liked to *read*. Pulp fiction authors were no-holds-barred entertainers—real storytellers. They were more interested in a thrilling plot twist, a horrific villain or a white-knuckle adventure than they were in lavish prose or convoluted metaphors.

The sheer volume of tales released during this wondrous golden age remains unmatched in any other period of literary history—hundreds of thousands of published stories in over nine hundred different magazines. Some titles lasted only an issue or two; many magazines succumbed to paper shortages during World War II, while others endured for decades yet. Pulp fiction remains as a treasure trove of stories you can read, stories you can love, stories you can remember. The stories were driven by plot and character, with grand heroes, terrible villains, beautiful damsels (often in distress), diabolical plots, amazing places, breathless romances. The readers wanted to be taken beyond the mundane, to live adventures far removed from their ordinary lives—and the pulps rarely failed to deliver.

In that regard, pulp fiction stands in the tradition of all memorable literature. For as history has shown, good stories are much more than fancy prose. William Shakespeare, Charles Dickens, Jules Verne, Alexandre Dumas—many of the greatest literary figures wrote their fiction for the readers, not simply literary colleagues and academic admirers. And writers for pulp magazines were no exception. These publications reached an audience that dwarfed the circulations of today's short story magazines. Issues of the pulps were scooped up and read by over thirty million avid readers each month.

Because pulp fiction writers were often paid no more than a cent a word, they had to become prolific or starve. They also had to write aggressively. As Richard Kyle, publisher and editor of *Argosy*, the first and most long-lived of the pulps, so pointedly explained: "The pulp magazine writers, the best of them, worked for markets that did not write for critics or attempt to satisfy timid advertisers. Not having to answer to anyone other than their readers, they wrote about human beings on the edges of the unknown, in those new lands the future would explore. They wrote for what we would become, not for what we had already been."

Some of the more lasting names that graced the pulps include H. P. Lovecraft, Edgar Rice Burroughs, Robert E. Howard, Max Brand, Louis L'Amour, Elmore Leonard, Dashiell Hammett, Raymond Chandler, Erle Stanley Gardner, John D. MacDonald, Ray Bradbury, Isaac Asimov, Robert Heinlein—and, of course, L. Ron Hubbard.

In a word, he was among the most prolific and popular writers of the era. He was also the most enduring—hence this series—and certainly among the most legendary. It all began only months after he first tried his hand at fiction, with L. Ron Hubbard tales appearing in *Thrilling Adventures, Argosy, Five-Novels Monthly, Detective Fiction Weekly, Top-Notch, Texas Ranger, War Birds, Western Stories,* even *Romantic Range.* He could write on any subject, in any genre, from jungle explorers to deep-sea divers, from G-men and gangsters, cowboys and flying aces to mountain climbers, hard-boiled detectives and spies. But he really began to shine when he turned his talent to science fiction and fantasy of which he authored nearly fifty novels or novelettes to forever change the shape of those genres.

Following in the tradition of such famed authors as Herman Melville, Mark Twain, Jack London and Ernest Hemingway, Ron Hubbard actually lived adventures that his own characters would have admired—as an ethnologist among primitive tribes, as prospector and engineer in hostile climes, as a captain of vessels on four oceans. He even wrote a series of articles for *Argosy,* called "Hell Job," in which he lived and told of the most dangerous professions a man could put his hand to.

Finally, and just for good measure, he was also an accomplished photographer, artist, filmmaker, musician and educator. But he was first and foremost a *writer,* and that's the L. Ron Hubbard we come to know through the pages of this volume.

This library of Stories from the Golden Age presents the best of L. Ron Hubbard's fiction from the heyday of storytelling, the Golden Age of the pulp magazines. In these eighty volumes, readers are treated to a full banquet of 153 stories, a kaleidoscope of tales representing every imaginable genre: science fiction, fantasy, western, mystery, thriller, horror, even romance—action of all kinds and in all places.

Because the pulps themselves were printed on such inexpensive paper with high acid content, issues were not meant to endure. As the years go by, the original issues of every pulp from *Argosy* through *Zeppelin Stories* continue crumbling into brittle, brown dust. This library preserves the L. Ron Hubbard tales from that era, presented with a distinctive look that brings back the nostalgic flavor of those times.

L. Ron Hubbard's Stories from the Golden Age has something for every taste, every reader. These tales will return you to a time when fiction was good clean entertainment and the most fun a kid could have on a rainy afternoon or the best thing an adult could enjoy after a long day at work.

Pick up a volume, and remember what reading is supposed to be all about. Remember curling up with a *great story*.

—Kevin J. Anderson

KEVIN J. ANDERSON *is the author of more than ninety critically acclaimed works of speculative fiction, including The Saga of Seven Suns, the continuation of the Dune Chronicles with Brian Herbert, and his* New York Times *bestselling novelization of L. Ron Hubbard's* Ai! Pedrito!

The Red Dragon

Chapter One

M Y dear Miss Sheldon, you must believe me when I say that Manchuria is no place for a lady!" Blakely patted a stray black hair in place and frowned for emphasis. "Even the thought of your being in that country alarms me."

Miss Betty Sheldon also frowned, though her eyes were more thoughtful than worried. Seated in the overstuffed armchair, she could look out over the roofs of Legation Street to the place where the Forbidden City gleamed red and yellow in the setting sun.

"Then," said Betty, in a low, vibrant voice, "I shall have to forego the pleasure of being a lady."

"You mean . . . you mean you're actually going to discard all my earnest advice and go along? Certainly you can't mean that! I understand, Miss Sheldon, that your father's death has left you greatly upset. You must place some faith in the judgment of others. You'd never be able to make the journey. The Japanese swarm over that country. There are bandits, and excessive hardships. There are long marches which are completely without water.

"I advise you once more, Miss Sheldon, to let me handle this. I will take the chart and go after the Black Chest. You need only to remain here in Peking while I make the journey.

Barring accidents, I should return within three months. After that, I am certain that you will have ample funds for your return to the United States."

Betty Sheldon gave Blakely a cool stare. He was tall and gaunt, and his hair was a sheet of black oilcloth glued to his skull. His shirt bore a wing collar, clean and starched, but his fingernails were filled with ancient, dry dirt. His eyes were brittle things which stared behind you, and never straight at you.

"Now let me get this straight, Mr. Blakely. You are to take the chart and bring the Black Chest to me at Peking. Then—"

"Then you will reward me with ten per cent of the sale price of the contents of this mysterious Black Chest and we'll call everything square."

Betty Sheldon shook her head in perplexity. Her corn-colored hair shimmered under the impact of a ray of light and her eyes were as unfathomable, as blue as the deepest portion of the sea. She was very little more than five feet three, and when Blakely climbed out of his chair and paced the room, she felt like Gulliver in Brobdingnag—smaller, in fact.

Blakely shook a bony finger under her small, pert nose and his voice sounded like an off-key baritone horn. "Miss Sheldon, I was young once myself. In fact, I am still young." He paused to brush imaginary dust from his black suit coat. "I know to what depths of folly the younger generation can stoop. This idea of yours is utterly ridiculous. You think—" he shook his finger again, and Betty thought she heard the bones rattle— "you think that you can saunter through Manchuria to this what-ever-it-is, dig a hole, pull out the Black Chest, and then saunter back through Manchuria and arrive in Peking intact. You think you could make your way, unaided, through a seething country, while having in your possession probably no less than a million dollars."

"I didn't say that the Black Chest was worth a million dollars," protested Betty from the depths of the chair.

"Well, no doubt it is. Perhaps it is worth more than that. I know it's valuable, or that old fool Sheldon—"

"I beg your pardon?"

"Eh? Oh, pardon *me*. That is what the natives called him. Anyway, Miss Sheldon, your father would never have risked his neck twice and yours once to try to get it out unless it was worth plenty. I'm convinced of that. He blew your entire fortune looking for it, didn't he?"

"That's beside the point, Mr. Blakely."

"Yes, to be sure. But once again, let me state that there are Japanese soldiers in that country. They are utterly lawless. They shoot on sight and kill for the sport of it. And then there are bandits who seek to wipe out every white person who arrives in their vicinity. Some of these bandits stand on rocks, like this." Blakely raised his arms and pretended to sight along a rifle. "And when they even see a dust cloud, they fire into it before they know who it is."

"Where are the sound effects?" asked Betty Sheldon.

"Sound effects! I am sure, young lady, that we were speaking of—"

"Never mind." She stepped away from the chair. Even with high heels and cocky hat she failed to reach his shoulder.

"Never mind going over it again, Mr. Blakely. They sent me here from the US Legation. They told me you were a collector, a man schooled in these things. That you were in a position to give me valuable advice."

"Of course I am!" cried Blakely, staring behind her and patting his hair. His mouth was slack, the lower lip protruding.

"But I find upon speaking to you that you are interested in only ten per cent of the Black Chest. You place your price at ten per cent. That was not clever of you—it is too little pay. Fifty per cent might have drawn me into a bargain. The ten only showed me that you had determined to cut me out completely. Please don't trouble me further, and please do not mention this business to anyone." She went to the door and placed her brown gloved hand on the knob.

"But where are you going?"

A small, wicked light came into being behind her eyes. "I think I shall ferret out the Red Dragon and see what he can offer me by way of a bargain."

Blakely tottered. He clapped a hand over his forehead and fumbled for his chair, still staring at her, jaw slack. "The . . . the Red Dragon?"

She smiled, triumphantly. "Yes. The Red Dragon."

"That devil! You'd . . . you'd actually trust your chart to the . . . the Red Dragon? But he's no better than a thief! A white thief in a yellow land. He's despicable!"

"Nevertheless, I am going." She jerked the door open.

"But . . . but you're not going to carry your chart about Peking with you?"

"It's safest with me, Mr. Blakely." Her heels clattered down the winding wooden steps as though a sergeant major sounded cadence for her. At the bottom she glanced back long enough to see Blakely's blanched face peering out his door.

At the curb she stopped, tapping one trim slipper against the ancient stone. Several rickshaws were drawn up there, shafts resting on the curb. The Chinese boys, bare of foot and naked of chest, drew away from her. Betty Sheldon frowned. These boys usually tried to tear a possible fare apart.

"Pete!" she called sternly.

No one moved in the rickshaw line. Uneasily she scanned them, suddenly realizing that her own boy, nicknamed Pete and hired by the week, was among the missing. She glanced up at the building front and saw that Blakely was watching from his window.

A rickshaw was trundled up from the back of the structure. It was black, trimmed with red, and its human horse was a mighty-chested Tartar. He slammed the shafts down in front of her and jerked his thumb toward the seat.

Dusk was gathering, and all along this thoroughfare dim lights were being lit. It was a dismal time of evening, and the silence that broods over the dead Imperial City was intensified by twilight. She was the only white person in sight. The Tartar once more jerked his thumb at the seat.

"Where b'long?" he rumbled.

She could feel Blakely's eyes boring into her slim, straight back. "Hotel du Pekin, and chop-chop. Savvy?"

"Uh-huh." The Tartar started off without waiting to see

whether or not she was properly seated. As an afterthought he glanced back and then, with a rolling clang of the bell, headed off to the north.

A block away from the office building, he stopped again. This time he lighted the paper lantern and hung it higher on the dash.

"Wait!" cried Betty when he picked up the shafts. "You're going the wrong way. Savvy? Hotel du Pekin that direction, east!"

He shook his head impatiently and headed north. Betty gasped and looked anxiously about her. The Tartar was almost seven feet tall, looming like a Percheron horse between the shafts. His stench was gagging.

Betty held a small swagger stick in her hand. For a moment she stared at it, and then, her eyes suddenly determined, she raised it and crashed a stinging blow into the Tartar's back. He shrugged as though a fly had touched him and trotted serenely on, still heading north.

Glancing around her, Betty knew that she was already lost. She would have to walk in circles until she struck a familiar street or landmark. Nevertheless, she stood up and tried to step out.

Feeling the change of weight on the shafts, the Tartar whirled. One great hand, twice as large as her face, crashed against her forehead. She slumped back, her ears ringing.

Still holding the shafts, the Tartar watched her for further rebellion. When her head was clear again, she once more lifted the stick. Her face was as white as ashes and her hand shook.

8

"Wait!" cried Betty when he picked up the shafts. "You're going the wrong way. Savvy? Hotel du Pekin that direction, east!"

The swagger stick, less than three ounces in weight, swished down at the Tartar's face. He caught it with a grunt and jerked it away from her. Using only one fist, he broke it neatly and cast it aside.

Resuming the shafts, the Tartar trotted serenely north. The streets were growing darker, as they had already gone beyond the civilized quarter into the dark alleys which lay hidden along the great outer wall.

In the darkest alley of them all, the Tartar stopped again and looked back at her. She remained quiet and composed, but her eyes were almost black with pent-up rage.

Setting down the shafts, the Tartar retreated a few steps and fished in his dirty open blouse for a cigarette. He started to apply the match.

Betty dropped from the rickshaw like a shot arrow. She hoped that she could at least make the larger street farther on before he caught up with her. Her high heels caught in the rough paving and hampered her. Sandals grated behind her. She heard the Tartar grunting as he ran.

Abruptly a filthy arm encircled her throat. She was lifted up bodily and planted against the wall. The Tartar grunted again, exhaling a sigh strong with garlic. His grip was unconsciously crushing her shoulder.

The sound of a motor came to them faintly and then grew in volume. Betty's heart began to hammer with hope. Perhaps the car would pass through this alley—and if it did, the traveler could see by the headlights that all was not well. Perhaps it would be an officer returning from the plains to Legation Street.

10

The headlights of the car blinded her, but she could see by the curved radiator that it was a Renault. Perhaps, then, it would be a French officer. She stared up into the Tartar's impassive face and a withering fear caught at her throat. The Tartar was not afraid. He merely stood there, waiting for the car to come up.

The brakes squealed and the car came to a halt beside her. A voice, dull like a rasp on wood, cut through the window. "Blindfold her, fool!"

The Tartar spun her about and grunted something in a Chinese dialect she did not understand. She heard footsteps on the running board and then on the pavement. Trying to turn her head, she felt the Tartar's grip tighten. She could not see who the newcomer was.

A rag was swiftly passed before her eyes and secured with unnecessary strength.

The white man rasped, "Search her! Thoroughly!"

Her words were like the twang of a fine steel blade. "You don't dare do that."

The Tartar's hand fastened on the back of her light dress. She felt his muscles tighten preparatory to a jerk.

The whiplash crack of a pistol rocketed through the alley. The Tartar's hand relaxed, then clawed at her shoulder. Betty stepped quickly aside. Something hot and wet was on her forearm. A hot, salty stench was in her nostrils. She ripped the bandage away from her eyes and whirled. The Tartar was writhing on the paving, spitting red fluid.

The white man behind her was suddenly a blur of action. He crouched. Something blue glinted in his hand. Before she

11

even recognized a gun, she struck it away. The shot crashed up against the stars.

The white man jumped back, swearing. He tried to direct the gun against her, but all the might in her two hands shoved up. The gun came free, but Betty knew that it was not her strength which had taken it.

Boot heels were pounding toward them. A crisp clear voice was shouting, "Drop that gun and stand up!"

The white man leaped for the running board. The engine roared and chattered as the gears went home. With a grinding squeal of tires the Renault shot away.

Two stabs of red flame came from the direction of the bootbeats. Glass rattled against the alley. The Renault went around a corner on two wheels and was gone from sight.

Betty leaned back against the wall, trying to catch her breath, suddenly weak and shaking. Everything was blurred for a minute. When she brought her chin up again, she saw that a slim gentleman, hazy in the starlight, stood before her, his head bared.

He bowed and clicked his heels. Even teeth glowed white as he said, "Pardon me, Miss Sheldon. I'm afraid my introductions are always abrupt."

She knew, then, that she was face to face with that almost legendary figure, the Red Dragon.

Chapter Two

HE took her by the arm and led her out to the wider street. Then, suiting his long stride to hers, he hurried through the shadows for two blocks. She recognized one end of Legation Street.

"Sorry to hurry you," he said, "but I didn't want us to be found with the Tartar back there. Lord knows, they've got enough on me now. Shall we find rickshaws?"

"No," said Betty with great emphasis. "I never want to see another! Let's walk, by all means."

"Good. I thought you might be too tired after your experience." He set an easy pace and, though he kept to the shadows of walls and steered clear of lights, his air was that of a gentleman out for an evening stroll after the heat of the day.

The conversation seemed to be over, but she didn't feel any strain in the silence. It was an easy, companionable thing. Walking with him past paper lanterns and iron gates through which flowers peered was so natural that her imagination played her a trick in making her feel that she had known this man for many, many friendly years.

Stealing an occasional glance sideways, she appraised him. His hat was soft and light gray, pulled low over one eye and tilted to the front. His coat was of dark blue material, well tailored. Below the coat, whipcord riding breeches and shining artillery boots didn't seem out of place.

He caught her looking at him once and smiled. She liked his eyes. They were as gray as his hat, and somehow as dark as his coat. She didn't know why that was. She felt that she had seen his face elsewhere, and then she recognized a dashing subject of an old master. His face was meant for an artist's canvas. It would try a painter's brush—that arrogant, whimsical, decisive expression. He had the appearance of a man who is born to be obeyed but who doesn't especially care. Something else caught her attention. The way his shoulders swung as he walked. A carefree swing, just as though a bullet might not come from the next alley, the next door, and cut off his existence—no, life—forever. He made her feel that everything was easy.

It was far to the Hotel du Pekin, and after half a mile of silent striding—of trying to match that swing of his with her slim, trim feet—her curiosity overcame her.

"Was that just coincidence?" she asked.

He glanced at her, smiling. "My getting there in the nick of time? No. Far from it, Miss Sheldon. I saw you get off the train at the North Gate this morning, and I followed you all through a long, dry day to see that these high binders didn't get you into trouble."

"But why all the interest in me?"

"There are many people interested in you just now."

"That's evading my question."

"Of course it is." He laughed, and after a brief pause, said, "Did you ever hear your father speak of me?"

"Once or twice. He always said that everyone was wrong about you."

"That was very kind of him. Three years ago, before you came over here from the States, your father gave me refuge in his camp when I was afoot and had a patrol after me. Of course he never dared speak of it to anyone—not even to you."

"That isn't the whole truth, is it?"

"No. Unfortunately, it isn't. I'm very interested in that mysterious Black Chest that your dad located up there in Manchuria. But I'm not asking any questions, and I don't want any information."

"Not unless I give it, free?"

"That's different. But after all, my reputation—"

"—is more aptly suited to a man named Blakely."

"Quite right. I'll agree with you perfectly on that. Old George Blakely was certainly born to be hanged, shot, or otherwise mangled. He'll get his one of these days, if I have to do it myself. He even knew that I was following you. How do you like that?"

"How do you know?"

"Well, he made a very elaborate show of having your rickshaw boy call around at the side entrance, and of course I spotted the boy and waited for you there. Until I saw George Blakely have his chauffeur run the Renault out, I didn't even know you had gone."

"So it was Blakely who had the Tartar take me to that place!"

"Yes. He wanted that chart or whatever it is you're carrying around with you, and he was quite willing to murder you to get it, after you refused it to him point-blank. We haven't heard the last of that fellow."

She liked the way he said "we." "Then you'll help me?"

"Certainly, if you feel that you can trust these so-called bad ethics of mine."

"Then what are we going to do?"

"Want my decision?"

"Certainly."

"We'll pack you out of Peking in something like two hours. First we'll call at the Hotel du Pekin and have something to eat. Then we'll go up to your room and pack."

"You mean you'll appear in public?"

"Why not? Few people know me by sight."

She felt something solid at his side and glanced down. Two .45 automatics were there, buckled low in black holsters, each one tied down securely for a quick draw. She had heard that gunmen of the old West did that. Instead of chilling her, they thrilled her.

"But don't forget this," he said. "You're doing something that everyone in Peking will tell you is utterly wrong. You're trusting the man known as the Red Dragon. Trusting a white renegade, a traitor and a thief."

Her answer was a laugh. One had only to look into his clear eyes and see him smile to know he could be trusted.

"I don't like to call you by such a wild title," said Betty. "What can I use?"

"Michael Stuart, if you wish. Or, if you don't like to say

16

Michael, you can say just plain Mike, or maybe Micky. Take your pick."

"Imagine anyone calling you Micky! I think Mike will be all right. It sounds nice and solid and—well, a bit tough."

"Of course it does. The one thing they haven't called me in China is the antonym for tough. Here's the hotel."

She didn't think that he would actually enter the place. She had heard that six governments wanted him, dead or alive, and that any one of them would pay well for his corpse. Japan alone had placed a hundred thousand yen—fifty thousand dollars—on his head. Of course it would take a brave man to get him, but a man properly doped with heroin might undertake it.

Suddenly she was appalled at herself. The Hotel du Pekin was such a respectable place, and she had always felt so dignified in it. And here she was, striding up the wide steps to the door on the arm of a man whose name was enough to turn out an army and a half-dozen gunboats. She swallowed hard and kept on going.

They crossed the lobby to the desk, and she was conscious of eyes. She looked up at his face and forgot about them.

"Miss Sheldon's key, please," he said.

The clerk stared at him, and then the metal jingled on the polished countertop. The key was pressed into her hand.

"I'll wait for you in the dining room, Miss Sheldon."

"All right—Mike."

At the bottom of the stairs she looked back and saw his broad, swinging shoulders disappear behind a potted palm.

Michael Stuart, the Red Dragon, found a table at the far

side of the room where he could sit with his back to the wall. He ran his fingers through his red-blond hair and scanned the room.

A Chinese waiter started toward the lobby door, glancing fearfully back at every fifth or sixth step. Michael Stuart smiled.

"Boy!" he called.

The waiter whirled. Under his long apron, his knees sent out ripples of fear. His eyes were black and wide. In a moment he collected himself and came back toward the table.

Stuart looked a hole through him, then motioned at a chair close by, beside the wall. "Sit down there," he said in Mandarin Chinese.

The Chinese wilted into the seat, staring and mutely pleading.

"Know me?" said Stuart, no longer smiling.

"Yes, master."

"Know what happens to people who know me?"

"Oh, yes, master."

"But you don't know me."

"Oh, no, master."

"See that you don't refresh your memory."

Ignoring the waiter, Stuart gazed again across the dining room. There were several parties there, but they were mostly people from the legations. All except that man—Stuart looked more closely at a Japanese gentleman who dined by himself. That man was . . . Stuart frowned, trying to remember.

It was . . . yes! That was Suga Jigoku Neko! Suga, the Hell-Cat!

Stuart thought rapidly. The presence of Suga Jigoku Neko in Peking meant but one thing. The Japanese had already hit the trail of the Black Chest, and they meant to garner it for themselves, if possible. Otherwise they would never send so accomplished a killer and so gifted a spy as Suga Jigoku Neko to Peking.

Suga, the Hell-Cat, glanced up and half rose from his chair. His face was taut, his eyes wide and black. One hand slunk down to his side.

Stuart's fingers snapped down and then up. A .45 automatic glittered amid the silver and crystal. Suga Jigoku Neko placed his hands, palms down, on the tablecloth. Stuart smiled, though the smile did not reach his eyes.

Something clicked in Stuart's brain. Glancing sideways, he stared at the empty chair. The waiter who knew him had disappeared.

Michael Stuart, the Red Dragon, holstered the gun and stood up. He strode carelessly across the checkered hardwood floor to the table of the Japanese.

"Pleasant greetings," said Stuart.

"*Oyasumi nasare.* Good evening," said Suga, listlessly.

"Death ever stalks the unwary," quoted Stuart.

Suga bent over his plate and shot a hard glance from the corner of his eye. "In the mouth of the lion, the lamb is but a tender morsel." To emphasize his point, Suga bit deep on a large piece of mutton. The gravy ran unheeded down his otherwise polished jowl. His bristly hair quivered.

Stuart knelt and deprived Suga of his gun. Throwing this

into a potted palm some feet away, he strode back to the lobby and mounted the stairs three at a time as soon as he was out of the Hell-Cat's sight.

On the third floor, he quickly scanned the numbers and then hammered with a hard fist on the panel. In a moment, Betty Sheldon opened it a crack and peered out. Recognizing him, she threw it wide.

He entered with a whirling motion and a smile. He bolted the door from the inside. "I never did like corridors. Pack up quickly, the Japanese have us spotted. We'll have to reach the Great Wall before they do, otherwise we'll never get through Jehol."

"You mean they're going to try to stop us?"

"No," he said brutally. "They're going to kill us if they get their hands on us. You've thrown your game over with me, Miss Sheldon."

She nodded, standing there against the door, dressed in an evening gown which sparkled in the light. She saw with a little alarm that his face was as hard as marble.

"You've thrown your lot with a renegade, and you're now as hunted as I am. If you ever want to realize your father's dream and bring the Black Chest out of that country, you'll have to stand by me in everything I do. But if you don't like that, there's the telephone. Call the United States Legation. Tell them that the Red Dragon is in your room. The Marines will do the rest."

She pressed herself back against the bolted panel, feeling somehow small before the great vitality of this man. A smile came to her firm, determined lips. She held out her hand.

Michael Stuart shook it, and the hardness dropped away from his face. Suddenly he laughed.

"Get your duds packed. Leave all this frilly stuff here, you won't need it in Manchuria. Got boots? Put them on. We'll have to ride all night. There are stars. That's a help."

He saw the boots under the bed and he dragged them out, smiling at their smallness. She pulled her breeches out of a trunk and went swiftly into the next room.

While she changed she could hear his quick, deft hands moving things about, and she knew that he was packing for her.

When she appeared, he glanced over her, noting the trim gabardine shirt and breeches, the well-cut short coat.

"You'll do," he said. "There are your bags. Leave a note to have them stored here for you, though I doubt whether you'll ever see them again. Have you any money down in the safe?"

She shook her head and pulled a small wallet from her jacket.

"That all the money you've got in the world?" he demanded.

"Two tens and a five—and in Mex, at that."

He chuckled. "You've certainly got your nerve, lady. You had no way of getting out of this country at all, and you couldn't even pay your bill here." The chuckle became a rolling, rollicking laugh.

He snatched his own wallet from his hip pocket and drew out two five-hundred-dollar Bank of Taiwan bills. "Take these, in case we get separated."

She knew that it was useless to protest, and so she took them and stored them away. He threw a hundred Mex on the table, for her hotel bill.

"All set?" he asked. "All right. Then stand close behind me,

21

and if the bullets fly, cut and run. I'll meet you at the North
Gate if things get too hot."

"You mean there may be a fight?"

"We'll have to work fast to get out at all." He started toward
the door.

Metal thundered on the wood before Stuart's face. He
backed up, his eyes as chill as blued steel. "The Japanese," he
said. "That's a gun butt banging on the door."

Her hands flew to her face and she shrank back. Michael
Stuart, the Red Dragon, stepped easily forward. Except for his
eyes, one would have thought him about to greet a welcome
guest.

Chapter Three

THE bolt on the door slid back noiselessly. Expecting violent action, Betty Sheldon felt her throat tightening. She saw that Stuart kept his hands away from his own guns. She saw him grasp the knob and turn it silently.

The gun butt thundered again on the panel once, twice. Stuart brought the door toward him with a swift pull. A red-tabbed, mustard-colored Japanese officer came suddenly into view, like a magician's stooge. Behind him the passage throbbed with yellow cloth and yellow faces. Betty saw all this in a split instant.

The gun butt was coming down for the third strike. The officer's fingers were tight on the barrel. Suddenly, with the door no longer there, the slanted eyes widened. The hand strove to arrest the downstroke of the gun, but it had already gone too far, too fast. The butt slapped straight and true into Stuart's outstretched hand.

Twisting the blue steel, Stuart jerked back. The muzzle covered them all as quickly and as neatly as though they had all been handicapped by leg irons.

"Good evening, gentlemen," said the Red Dragon, in English.

Suga Jigoku Neko shifted far behind the rest, a shrill exclamation on his lips.

The officer who had owned the gun was staring stupidly deep into the black tunnel. He gazed emptily into his palm and turned it over dazedly. The gesture made Betty want to laugh.

One soldier, quicker-witted than the rest, began to shove his way to the front. Using rifle butt and bayonet, he cleared his own path. Stuart was unmoving. The others watched sideways, fascinated.

When the Japanese soldier was within three feet of the door, Stuart's voice lashed out like a whip. *"Fusagu, tsuwamono.* Stop, soldier. All of you, listen. I give you three to disappear from this door. Then I begin to shoot. One—"

But the soldier only snorted. He raised his bayonet and leveled it for a thrust. The light had not stopped flickering on the naked steel when Stuart shot. The bullet slid off the gun and smashed through the soldier's chest. He sagged back, throwing out his arms.

The sound of the shot broke the spell. Revolvers leaped into view. Other soldiers began to press in.

Without moving, Stuart coolly emptied the gun into the press. In contrast to the others, he seemed self-possessed, emotionless.

The officer that had owned the gun pitched headfirst through the door and sprawled in front of Betty, his red tabs redder, his swarthy face ashen. He rolled over on his side, clawing at his pocket. He managed to draw a gun halfway out before Betty yanked it away from him.

Someone in the passage screamed, *"Akai Tatsu!* The Red Dragon!"

24

*The bullet slid off the gun and smashed through
the soldier's chest. He sagged back, throwing out his arms.*

Sprawling away, falling over one another, they tried to clear the corridor. Suga Jigoku Neko stopped long enough to shoot a clip over his shoulder, and then scurried out of sight down the stairway.

Both automatics ready in his fists, Stuart crouched low, unwilling to shoot men in the back as they strove to get away. Betty, pressed against the far wall, gun dangling from a nerveless hand, watched the silhouette he made in the doorway.

Suddenly he whirled.

"Grab that bag and come on—we'll have to make it fast!"

She stepped gingerly over the dead Japanese officer and then ran past Stuart. He took the bag from her and pulled her into position behind him. Then he sprinted for the steps and looked down, making certain that they were clear.

"All right. Now walk slow, understand?" He holstered both guns and took her arm. They walked sedately down toward the two potted palms at the foot of the staircase.

When they came into view of the lobby, the place was empty. Chairs were overturned, where guests had hurriedly departed. The desk was deserted. Newspapers were strewn about the reading table.

They went out of the great double doors and stopped. Looking down at the driveway, Stuart pointed to an American machine. "We'll take that one."

Expecting to see a grim visage, Betty glanced up. He was smiling and his eyes were amused.

Throwing the grip in back, Stuart started the engine and they pulled away at a snail's pace, headed south.

"Wait!" cried Betty. "The North Gate is the one we want. The trains!"

"I know, but they won't think we have nerve enough to catch a train right out of Peking."

They rounded a corner, and another corner, then Stuart's foot went down hard against the floorboards and stayed there. The speedometer needle went all the way over. Stuart's hands were light on the wheel, and no matter how loud the tortured rubber shrieked, his face did not change. Rocketing through the narrow, curving streets, they brushed disaster, and missed it by split inches.

Betty stared at the speedometer needle. It said one hundred. She swallowed hard, her senses reeling, and then recalled that all speedometers read in kilometers here and realized they were making sixty miles an hour.

It required an hour in a rickshaw to go from the Hotel du Pekin to the station at the North Gate, but the car made it in six minutes by the panel clock.

They drew up before the platform. Stuart took a twenty-dollar bill and shoved it behind the seat, where the owner would eventually find it. In the dust on the windshield he scrawled, "Thanks from the Red Dragon."

Beggars swarmed out at them exhibiting sores and maimed limbs. Stuart drew a massive handful of coppers from his pocket and flung them some distance to the side. The way before them was left quite clear.

A grunting, puffing engine stood beside the station, with its string of English-designed coaches. According to the bulletin board in the room where Stuart bought the tickets, it was scheduled to leave at seven that evening. It was now eight.

"We'll be off in a moment," he told Betty. "They always have to be an hour late, so they can try to make it up—which they never do."

"But maybe the Japanese—"

"Forget it. If they're coming, they're coming, that's all." He smiled. "No use getting gray hairs worrying about things. If they happen, they happen. Ninety per cent of the things people worry about never come off anyway. See that first class coach there? Go in and hold down one of the compartments until I get there."

Stuart moved away, and she climbed into the coach, boosting the bag in ahead of her.

The engineer sat high up on his seat, dozing and waiting for the station master to make up his mind about the departure of the night train, when a soft voice speaking Chinese woke him.

"Tonight," said the voice, "the Red Dragon rides with you. All speed is necessary. You will stop two miles south of Nankou without looking back, and you will immediately forget that you have stopped, or that you have ever seen me."

The engineer jerked upright, goading his nerve to look at the platform at the side of the cab. When he finally did so, the platform was empty. He shuddered and bawled strident orders to his black and greasy fireman.

A moment later, Michael Stuart entered the compartment and sat down beside Betty. He pulled down the shades until only an inch remained at the bottom. Then he offered her a cigarette and lit it for her. Puffing at his own, he lay along the leather seat and pried the window up a notch. Then he took a gun from its holster and leveled it very carefully.

The engine had begun to snort. The slack was being taken up in the cars. The headlights of a machine slashed over the train and a car stopped beside the platform.

Betty peered through her curtain and pulled nervously at the handle of her grip. The men were running toward the train, shouting and waving rifles.

The cars jerked, almost throwing Stuart off the seat. Another jerk, and the station began to move away from them. The shouts were louder. One of the men reached for the rail and managed to place one foot on the vestibule.

Stuart leaned out and chopped down with one shot. The man fell off screaming, blood spurting from his fingers. The station was gone from sight.

With a sigh Stuart sat up and replaced the automatic. "Here we go," he said. "And now, for the first time, I think we'd better get a few things straight. We'll have plenty to worry about before this night is over, let me tell you."

Betty dragged at the forgotten cigarette and leaned back, bringing her small feet up under her. Looking at her, Stuart realized that she was beautiful. He had never noticed how delicately molded her features were! But she looked tired.

"Maybe you'd rather sleep," he said.

"Not I, I'm having the time of my life. I'll be either a very wise lady or a nervous wreck by the time I get out of this thing."

"I think the Black Chest is worth it. Tell me, how did you ever get the map and get away when your father was killed?"

"That's one of the oddest things that ever happened to me. I went up to this country with Dad a few months ago, as you've probably heard. I wasn't feeling very fit for a few days—fell off a horse—and Dad thought he'd better send me back to the nearest town.

"I had been carrying the chart for him, because he thought it was safer with me than with him. And when I was sent back, he was so worried about me that he completely forgot to take the chart away with him. I waited for some little while for word from him—"

"Skip that part," Stuart said, sympathetically.

"No, it's all right. I get a funny lump in my throat when I think about it. Sorry. Anyway, Mike, I heard that bandits had gotten him and had taken all the baggage, and I came down to Peking to get help.

"I had no money, and I thought I could raise some on the strength of this chart. You know the rest." She pulled a locket away from her white throat and gave it to him. "See the back? Scratched in the soft gold? That's the chart."

"You shouldn't show it to me."

"Aren't we partners?"

He grinned, and regarded the scratched map. "And this is the key to whatever is so valuable in the famous Black Chest. Well, with luck we'll get through the Japanese lines north of the Wall and find out all about it." He gave the locket back to her.

"I suppose you'll think I'm pretty curious and ain't had no bringin' up, Mike, but what—how—?"

"How did I ever become the notorious Red Dragon? That's

easy, and it's kind of silly, but so long as we're swapping secrets, I might as well own up to it and tell you. You'll be the first person who ever knew besides myself."

She smiled at him and drew her feet further up. Far back in the corner, she watched him, and listened to the song of steel wheels on steel rails.

"You see, I'm not really the Red Dragon anymore," he said. "Once upon a time, there was a real reason for the Red Dragon, but not now. The Japanese stole it."

"Stole it?"

"Sure. A power that I'll never be able to name—"

"Why not?"

"You're worse than a kid."

Michael Stuart pushed his gray felt hat up on the back of his head and put his boot heels on the opposite seat.

"You see, Betty, nations are like old maids. The older they get, the more careful they think they have to be about their reputations. I swore that I'd never divulge the name of the country, and I won't now, even though they threw me down when I needed them most.

"Several years ago—not so long, either—I was a self-respecting officer of the United States Marine Corps. Just a second-rate second looie, but an officer and gentleman just the same. But it got on my nerves, and I resigned. Then this thing came up, and I knew my Chinese, having been a USMC language student right here in Peking.

"I'll tell you what they wanted to do, Betty. It was one of the wildest schemes a flock of fat politicians—pardon me, I mean dignified statesmen—ever thought up. They wanted to

31

set up China as an empire again. They wanted to select their own king or emperor, and then they could have all the China trade and the whole works, see?"

"Yes. Sounds like a good idea."

"It is a good idea, and darned good business, too. China needs a strong government and they were fixing to give China just that. Take this demonstration tonight. Japanese soldiers in Peking, the Imperial City. Japan would never dare pull anything like that if China were on her feet."

Stuart sank further down, and the seatback pushed his hat loosely over one eye. He studied the glowing end of his cigarette.

"So all they needed was an emperor, and they thought that would be easy. Little old Henry Pu Yi was the boy. Yessir. Little old Henry would make a darned good emperor. Easy to handle, you see.

"But unfortunately, when the Imperial City first fell, Henry was whisked away to the Japanese Legation at Tientsin. And he was there when I took this job over. I was supposed to whip up a lot of sentiment for the Imperial Dynasty, and I proceeded to do so. Hence the Red Dragon—that's the symbol of Imperial China. The natives thought the name pretty good, because I have hair that looks red in the sunlight. So that's what they called me, and I did a lot of campaign stunts for the country that hired me.

"My next job on the program was very simple. All I had to do was to kidnap Henry Pu Yi out of the Japanese hands at Tientsin and shove him on the throne in Peking.

"All started off fine, but unfortunately I made too good

a show of it, and the Japanese, being artists one way and another, copied me and stole my stuff." He waved his cigarette at her and cocked his head on the side.

"Do you know what they did?" he said. "They took old Henry up to Manchuria. They bought out some warlords, killed some others off, and created the Empire of Manchukuo. Henry, so to speak, sold out to the Japanese right when he was about to become the head of his own country. So now he manages the Manchukuo farce—under Japanese supervision."

Michael Stuart sighed and lit another cigarette. He blew out the match and continued in the same breath: "I was immediately dropped by the country that hired me. I was disowned completely and left, broke and helpless, to shift for myself.

"Now here's the tough part. I can't go to any seaport in China—not one! And I can't get across the Russian border. And I can't—oh, well, you see how it is. I'm trapped in the center of one of the biggest countries in the world. Trapped, that's all."

She noticed that, while he spoke, his face became haggard, like that of a man who has tried long to do a thing only to fail once more. But he brightened after a moment.

"So," he said, "I did myself proud as the Red Dragon. Whenever somebody is getting a raw deal, I try to step in and help him out. I've done the spectacular, so that my name would be a help in itself. I've even robbed banks and sent the proceeds into flood-ravaged areas in the north. The funds I took from the banks would have stayed there until doomsday. They had been sent from the United States, and they never got any further than a bank vault. It's things like that which have made me a bad name."

Her eyes were damp with sympathy. "And there's no way you can escape?"

"Only one way."

"And that?"

"Is via the old grim reaper."

She sat up straight, her face white. Stuart laughed.

"Don't worry about me. They'll catch me one of these days and cut off my head and hang it on a pole, and that will be the end of the Red Dragon. There were heads on poles in Morrison Street in Peking. Did you see them?"

She shuddered and sank back. "Maybe if we get enough money for the Black Chest—"

"Stay the thought. All the money in the world can't buy my way. I know. I've tried it. I'm trapped in the middle of China, and I'll be here from now on until they lay me six feet under, sans my skull—and even then I'll still be here. Let's talk about something pleasant."

"About what we'll do if they stop this train in Nankou, for instance," said Betty.

"We won't be on it. They'll stop it all right, and we're near there right now. We'll have to run the risk of getting away and across the Wall from the open plains. That's all we can hope to do. It's going to be tough going."

The train slowed down and, peering out, Betty saw the lights of a faraway city which would be Nankou.

"He's stopping for us," said Stuart. "This is our stop. We'll make it through the window."

With a squeal and hiss the train lurched to a stop. Stuart smiled at Betty and then pulled up a window. He boosted her through and tossed the bag after her. He set one leg over the sill and was about to drop when a voice in the door stopped him.

"One moment, Red Dragon."

Stuart pulled himself sideways and turned. He was staring into an automatic barrel which looked as big as a railway tunnel. The barrel was shaking a little. Above it was the face of George Blakely.

"Well?" said Stuart.

"I never liked to shoot a man in the back," said Blakely, "and I wanted the pleasure of having you know that I heard every word you said, by listening at the ventilator of the next compartment. I knew that you would take this train."

Stuart felt Betty outside tugging at his boot, urging him to hurry. Blakely's finger started the short trek down the slack of his trigger.

Chapter Four

IN his smoking steel cab, the engineer was obeying orders. The Red Dragon had commanded that the train stop for one brief instant, and the Red Dragon was not a man to take excuses. From the Great Wall to Canton, wise Chinese followed his orders—too many of their number had already gone to their ancestors.

Without looking back, the engineer threw off the air brakes and cracked the throttle wide open. The wheels spun on the slippery rails and then, like a goaded bull, the engine jumped ahead.

Blakely, his greedy eyes filled with triumph, held his sights on Stuart's chest. Abruptly, the floor beneath his feet jerked, throwing him off balance. Blakely snatched wildly at the door, trying to level the gun even as he went down. He struck his oilcloth hair against the wood, rumpling it over into his eyes. When he had swept it away, the Red Dragon was gone.

Hoarse with rage, Blakely yanked at the overhead line which would signal the engineer to stop. He pulled it once, twice, three times, bracing himself against the gathering lurch of the wheels over the uneven roadbed.

But the engineer had heard the Red Dragon speak out of nowhere, and the train rocketed on across the plains until it was nothing more than a red pinpoint in the dark and a low murmur which dwindled away to nothing.

Stuart dusted the knees of his riding breeches and picked up Betty's grip.

"What was the matter?" she wanted to know.

"Caught my coat on a nail," Stuart said evenly. "Now the point is, where do we go from here?"

"You're the boss of the expedition," said Betty.

Stuart looked in the darkness at the white blur that was her face. He smiled and struck out at right angles to the track.

They walked on plowed ground and the deep furrows impeded them. Stuart bumped into a shrine and drew his light out of his pocket, flashing it inside the squat structure. A fat little god grinned at them.

"Good omen," Stuart said. "He's the deity of travel and fortune. Must be a road right beside here."

Betty laughed, nervously. "He's cute." Fumbling in her pocket, she found a match and lit it. A tuft of half-burned joss stood in an earthen vase beside the figure. She touched it off and sniffed at the rolling cloud of sandalwood which drifted out.

"That was very good, Betty. As soon as you lit it, the god pointed out a lighted window about two hundred yards up that way. See it?"

"Yes."

"It happens that this district had a famine last year. I saw to it that fifteen tons of wheat were brought in and distributed. For the moment we're on safe ground."

"Where did you get the wheat?"

"It was consigned in freight cars to the government down at Nanking. I borrowed it. Let's go."

He turned and looked north at the patch of glow that marked Nankou. He knew that this country here would be combed thoroughly in about an hour by Chinese troops.

The hut with the lighted window was square and built of yellow mud-blocks. It stood by itself, but a short distance behind it another set of buildings was dimly outlined against the sky.

Stuart rapped softly on the door and then stood back. For a few moments nothing happened. Then there came the slippety-slop of loose sandals against a dirt floor. A round face, incredibly dirty, was thrust at them.

"Good evening," Stuart said, speaking in the local dialect. "Is all well with your house?"

The Chinese looked at the girl and then saw that she was white. He started to slam the door, but Stuart blocked the move with his boot. His voice was edged, as he said, "Have a care, Ancient. It is the Red Dragon."

The Chinese backed swiftly from them, letting the door swing wide, displaying a squalid room littered with pans and clothing. The light came from a tallow candle on the table beside the bed. Stuart looked closely at the couch and saw that it held an old woman whose face was the shade and texture of white parchment.

"Your wife is ill?" Stuart asked.

Still jolted out of his wits, the Chinese could only nod.

39

"What is the cause?"

The Chinese swallowed hard, and then sang out, "It is a fever of the devils that our little house gods are powerless to drive away."

Stuart opened the grip and carried it to the table. Over his shoulder, he said to Betty, "I packed the contents of your medicine chest, and I think there may have been some aspirin in it." He pulled a flat box from the bag and shook it.

"My charm," said Stuart, "is stronger than that of all devils."

"It is known," murmured the Chinese, listening to the rattling box.

"In this case are white pellets of magic. They will make your wife well. Tell her that the Red Dragon has so decreed it. These white pellets will cause her to sweat mightily. Keep her covered well, and give her two each hour. By dawn the fever will be broken."

That the Chinese believed him implicitly was easily read in the slanting black eyes. He bobbed his shaven skull and bowed, murmuring thanks. "We have not yet forgotten what the Red Dragon has already done for us. That day, with food, you saved my sons and my house. Command me, Red Dragon, and I will obey."

Stuart bent over the old woman lying on the unclean, padded quilts and felt her wrist. He nodded.

"I know that the devils will be driven forth from her." Straightening, he said, "But the white pellets will not work in the presence of the Red Dragon. I must be far from this spot before they can be administered. I want ponies, two of them, and saddles and a bag of food."

"They are yours. Even my house, should you require it, is yours. I go immediately to obey." The Chinese padded through the door and went down the trail toward the mud barns.

From some distance away they could hear the Mongol ponies champing and crunching hay, but when their footsteps could be heard in the barn the crunching stopped.

"They are not good beasts," said the Chinese. "They are down from Mongolia, and all the devils of heaven are in them. You must exercise care, Red Dragon. But they will carry you far, if your weight remains heavy against their spines."

From a peg he dragged two saddles and a pair of scanty blankets, which he quickly turned over, exposing their under side. Stuart took them from him, aware of the fearful light which came across the Chinese face. Turning them, Stuart found an insignia emblazoned upon one of them. English letters. "D. R. S."

He thrust it before Betty Sheldon's eyes. "What do those initials mean?"

Betty gasped, and stumbled back.

"There is no cause for fear," said Stuart. "They stand for Daniel Randolph Sheldon, your father. Is that right?"

"Yes," she whispered. "All of his men were equipped with those saddle blankets."

"And he had about a hundred men, that right?"

"Yes."

Stuart turned back to the Chinese and threw the pocket torch on the blanket. "Where did you get this?"

"I did not steal it, Red Dragon. Truly, I did not steal it!"

"You know enough of me to understand that theft is not a major crime. I repeat, where did you get this?"

The Chinese averted his face. "Last month many soldiers came here with guns."

"What soldiers were they?"

"Japanese, Red Dragon. They came down from the Wall, raiding. Outside my fields they met a force of Chinese, and they fought for two days. As soon as the Japanese lost their horses, they entrenched themselves and fought bitterly, till they were driven back across the plains and over the Wall."

"And?"

"Some of the horses escaped the bullets and ran away. I found four without saddles, and after the battle was over I went out across the plains, selecting suitable equipment for these. I do not like the insignia of Japan, and when I found this saddle blanket I was delighted. I brought it here, and I have been afraid."

"But," said Stuart, "you need have fear no longer. I take it with us."

The Chinese stepped to the door. Trained as he was in the sounds of night, his keen ears detected a sound which had not yet reached either Stuart or Betty.

"Quickly!" said the Chinese. "Horsemen come! If they find you here—"

Stuart lunged into a stall and threw the initialed blanket across a pony's back. He strapped the light Cossack saddle over it and fought to place the bit between the horse's teeth. He led the stamping animal back to Betty and, catching hold of her heel, boosted her into the saddle.

The Chinese was preparing Stuart's horse. The hoofbeats were clearly audible now, like dull thunder. Stuart emptied the contents of the grip into two saddlebags and threw them across the pony's rump. He vaulted lightly into the saddle and turned, tossing a Bank of Taiwan bill to the Chinese. Then he rapped Betty's horse with the flat of his hand, and the beast shot away across the field, head down, scraggly mane flying.

They raced for half a mile; then Stuart drew in and listened. He could still hear the sound of running horses. That meant that several patrols were out, combing the terrain for any sign of the Red Dragon. Blakely had tipped them off, no doubt. The Red Dragon decided that Blakely's score had mounted too high and would demand an early settlement.

Betty stopped and listened, then slapped the reins against her pony's withers and galloped on beside Stuart. Riding low in the saddle, she could look between the pony's ears and sight the North Star. The horse was the right size for her, she decided. Her father had always used Western horses—big, powerful brutes. He had forbidden her to ride the Mongols because they were a vicious, treacherous breed. This pony came up to her shoulder, and she was five feet three. His head was a perfect rectangle, and the only thing massive about him was his jaw.

She found that she also liked the Cossack saddle. It was nothing more than two wooden crosstrees separated by a thin, belted leather cushion, but it was comfortable. No wonder the Cossacks were such good trick riders. To stand up, they only had to place the cushion belt over their toes and they were anchored. And to swing off one side and then back on at a dead run would be simple, with these crosstrees to use for leverage.

She felt heady, exhilarated with the keen tang of the night wind whipping her face and the knowledge that at any moment they might blunder into a patrol. The sight of Stuart, riding straight in his saddle beside her, was enough to make her senses spin with a new, indescribable sensation.

The North Star swerved a little as Stuart changed his course. She saw the white patch of his face as he looked back to make certain that she was all right and still with him.

The ground began to ascend under the pounding hoofs. The horses were shod and the metal struck fire from the flinty rocks of the hillside. The North Star hovered an instant, perilously, on the brink of the mountain which raised itself ahead of them, then it dove out of sight, leaving a black void between the pony's ears.

The ridge of the first range was as sharp as a knife. They plunged down a perpendicular bank, then raced up a second rise, topping it with a speed which took the girl's breath. After that she lost count. They were on the southern slope of the Western Hills—that much she knew. And they were now north of Nankou.

This was the northernmost part of what is called China proper. Beyond it was Jehol, in Japanese hands for the last year. Beyond Jehol lay Manchuria and the Black Chest.

Ahead, the skyline was jagged, but when Betty looked intently she saw that the jaggedness had a regularity to it.

It appeared to be the rampart of a feudal castle. Then she recognized what it must be.

Stuart pulled in to let his horse breathe. Pointing at the jagged line, he said, "We're standing on the last of China, Betty. Over there, whether they call it that or not, is Japan."

"Don't they patrol that border?"

"Certainly they do—and it has been patrolled for some hundreds of years. We're up against something now. That Wall is about thirty feet high and twenty feet across, and it extends for fifteen hundred miles, from the sea to the Russian border."

"I know. But why are we up against it?"

He turned in his saddle and threw one leg over the pommel. "It was built to keep the nomad tribes out of China, and it did so for over a thousand years, but if it was strong enough and high enough to keep those agile warriors out, then it's certainly going to make a stab at keeping us in."

"I thought there was a camel pass along here."

"There is. But it will be guarded, you can bet on that. If we're lucky, we'll find a postern in this side of the Wall. That will get us up to the top very nicely."

Suddenly she knew what he was driving at. "But the horses!"

He nodded. "We might be able to take the drop on the other side without getting hurt, but if you drop a horse thirty feet there's bound to be a splash. It would appear, Betty Sheldon, that we'll presently be afoot in Jehol, and a man who's afoot in that country can't ask any blessing from either the Japanese or the bandits—or from Blakely."

"Blakely!"

"Let it pass."

"I won't let it pass," said Betty. "You're keeping things from me. Blakely was on that train!"

"Of course he was, and he's up here trying to stop us. He'll go to almost any length to get the Black Chest. And he seems to be in with the Japanese somehow or other. But I don't quite get that part of it."

"What will happen if we walk into a Japanese patrol?"

Stuart shrugged against the starlight. "Search me."

"I thought they had some sort of a price on your head."

"Somebody was kidding you."

Betty snorted a very unladylike snort and sat up straight in her saddle, like a general in miniature. "Michael Stuart, you're keeping things from me because you think I'm too soft or something of the sort. Am I or am I not your partner?"

"You are my partner," said Stuart with a grin. "And you're a lady as well. All right, I'll tell you the truth. The Japanese will pay one hundred thousand yen for me dead or alive, preferably dead. I accidentally stopped their advance into Jehol about a year ago, and they didn't like it. Since that time, I've tangled with them. Now, after tonight, they'll be all the hotter on my trail. I think I killed a couple fellows up in the hotel, and the Japanese never did okay that."

"You had better not cross into their territory or they'll try to collect that hundred thousand," Betty said.

"They've been trying to collect it for eight months. You see, I'm sort of holding up their advance into China. It's not quite true, but almost. I took a prisoner when they got into

Jehol, and he's being kept down near Peking by a friend of mine."

"Who was it?"

"Oh, a member of their general staff. I told them he would be held as a hostage, in case they decided to step across the Wall in force. He's a brother of General Shimokado, who's holding down the forces in Manchuria and holding up Henry Pu Yi. You see, unfortunately this officer tried to get out of the place we were keeping him in and got caught by his coat collar on the wall pickets and strangled to death. It's all rather silly, you see."

"And they don't know what happened to him?"

"No. They'd pay very good money to know whether or not he is still alive. Shimokado, for family reasons, refuses to spare forces to the Jehol expedition—which is under a separate head—and so the attack is stalled off. I expect General Chang and his Chinese regulars will be in shape in a month or so and then I'll break the news to the Japanese and have a good laugh on their expense account."

Stuart placed his foot back in the stirrup and headed for the Wall at a slow walk. Betty fell in behind. A canyon lay between them and the frowning masonry, and at its bottom, Betty looked up to discover that the Wall followed a ridge and seemed a mile in the air.

Dismounting at the base, Stuart walked cautiously along, feeling for a postern. Betty could hear a stone rattle occasionally as he moved. She stared up at the Wall, remembering all she knew about it.

This particular stretch had been built last, and it was the

best. A million workmen had constructed ten miles of its curving, swooping length in ten days. Sixty per cent of them had died, and their bodies had been thrown into the Wall itself, for lack of time for proper burial. Six hundred thousand dead men were in the structure that confronted her. She winced, shivering, and turned away to find some solace in the glittering constellations overhead. But she could find no interest in them. Every time Stuart rattled a stone she jumped. She wondered if they would ever manage the ascent of this barrier. Its smooth sides were impossible to climb.

Stuart came back with a weary sigh. "No posterns, little lady. I don't know how we can do it. After daylight it will be impossible to keep out of sight here."

She clutched his arm. "Wait! What was that?"

The sound came to them again. The scrape of leather against pavement. Someone was on top of the Wall!

Chapter Five

"D ON'T move," Stuart whispered. "Maybe he hasn't heard us."

"Then you think it's a Japanese soldier?" she breathed.

"Yes, it must be. And if it is, there are others close by. Somebody may collect that hundred thousand yen tonight."

"Don't!" she pleaded.

Stuart drew a gun from his belt and leveled it at the Wall. He knew that if he shot, he'd bring men down upon them in a swarm, but a gun butt is always a good weapon in hand-to-hand combat.

A hissing voice floated to them. *"Dare aru?* Who is it?"

Betty's hand shook on Stuart's arm. She could see the bulk of the man above them against the sky, and she supposed that she could be seen as clearly.

Stuart's voice was squeaky but somehow hard. *"Suga Jigoku Neko.* Suga, the Hell-Cat, *de tayori.* With information."

The sentry grunted and stepped out of sight. He came back after a moment and something slithered down the side of the Wall.

"Koko aru nawa-hashigo. Here is a rope ladder."

"Don't go," Betty whispered. "He'll kill you as soon as he sees who it is!"

Stuart stepped away from her and grasped the hemp. He

49

went up swiftly, though the sagging crossbars were hard to keep underfoot. Grasping the rim of the Wall, he raised himself up and over with a single lunge.

The sentry saw him against the sky, saw that he confronted a big man who was either a Chinese or a foreigner. His bayoneted rifle snapped level. He raised his foot and then slammed it down far ahead of him. The bayonet was a brief flicker of light lancing square at its human target.

Stuart knew what was coming. No Oriental uses a bullet where a knife will serve, and this Oriental was utilizing Western tactics with his bayonet play. Stuart knocked the glitter aside. The catch of the bayonet rasped against his thumb.

The steel flickered again, and the Japanese retrieved his weapon for another swift lunge. But even in the semidarkness he could see that the knife was no longer affixed to the barrel. He stopped for a fraction of a second. It took only that length of time for Stuart to reverse the weapon and plunge it into the man's throat. The rifle clattered down on the pavement of the Wall.

Stuart stepped easily to the ladder head. "Pass up the saddlebags, and turn the horses loose without their bridles."

Stones rolled below, and then there came two sharp slaps close together. The ponies darted away and the rope ladder began to jerk. Stuart leaned down and helped Betty over the edge, taking the saddlebags from her shoulders.

"Where is the soldier?" she breathed.

"In warrior heaven by this time, I hope. I'm sorry, but I had to do it. I don't like knives."

"And now we're afoot in Jehol. What can we do about it?"

50

"I don't know yet. There's a watchtower up ahead—see it?" He pointed at the vague square bulk to the east. "We'll take a look from that."

They walked ahead, their boot heels making more noise than they had imagined they would. Fifty feet from the tower, Stuart stopped and set down the saddlebags.

"This Wall," he said, "is usually deserted. But tonight we've got to take every precaution. There seems to be a reception committee waiting for us every time we turn around."

Drawing an automatic, he stepped gingerly toward the tower, holding Betty behind him with his left hand.

"Seems to be empty," he whispered. "Pick up the bags back there and we'll scout the other side."

She did his bidding, but before she could get back to him, the Wall to the east blazed with powder flame. Slugs sang off the stone like an anvil chorus gone mad. Betty dropped to her knees and then pressed her face against the pavement, hoping that the horizontal leaden sleet would pass over her. She glanced up long enough to see that the Red Dragon was standing like a duelist, a gun in each hand, striving to give shot for shot with a bitter coldness that sent a chill down her spine.

She wanted to help him, but she knew that she would only hinder his efforts. She hitched herself over into the shelter of an embrasure and crouched there, trying to keep calm, trying to keep from being deafened by the racketing gun reports.

Stuart's left gun was empty before the right. He stepped aside, trying to change the clip. He didn't know what he had walked into. His own shots had blinded him, and the night

51

was a series of dancing red blobs. But if he could not see, he reasoned that neither could the Japanese soldiers.

Rifles he judged the weapons to be. That would mean soldiers, all right. It was going to be a better party than he had thought. He couldn't retreat because men might be behind him, and he couldn't drop thirty feet into a gully and leave Betty behind. He looked back, trying to see her, but the red blobs were in his way.

He thought that he might step back, but a concerted howl rose up before him and the firing stopped. Boot leather scraped on stone. Equipment clattered against the embrasures. It was like trying to shoot blindfolded. Stuart was not even certain which way the Wall went.

But the Japanese were under no such disadvantage. They charged like a black avalanche straight at the source of the shots. They knew it could not be anyone but the Red Dragon. Two .45 automatics had marked him. No other man in all China carried two .45s.

One word stood out of the howl as though painted in flame against the sky. *"Korosu! Korosu!* Kill! Kill!"

Another voice, a raucous whine, was like a knife through the shouts. *"Akai Tatsu!* Get him!"

That, Stuart knew, was Blakely.

Left gun reloaded, Stuart stepped back and into the center of the pavement. It seemed to take them so long to reach him. He planted both feet solidly and waited, slightly crouched. He raised up his hand and turned his coat collar up, so they couldn't see the white of his shirt. Wouldn't they ever reach him?

The black before him began to swirl. Stuart fired as fast as his fingers could press the triggers. The hot barrels scorched his fingers as he reversed them.

A soldier leaped at him, teeth bared. He dropped with a split skull. Another tried to close in from the right. Stuart sidestepped like a boxer and used his gun butt.

Hands clawed at him. Feet kicked out. Stuart was forced back against an embrasure. The press of bodies made him stagger into the cleft. His arms ached from giving and taking blows.

A rifle came at him against the sky. His chest caved under the impact. For a split instant he thought he had been shot, and then he knew he'd been struck by the butt. He tried to lean forward. The butt hit him again, its steel-shod weight pressing him further back.

He fought to keep his balance. For one second he thought he had succeeded. His foot went back into the night, into emptiness. Thirty feet of reedy black void sucked at him, carried him down.

He landed like a cat, rolled through thorns and brush, and came up against a rock. He stayed there for an instant, unable to rise. Above him he could see the flash of guns, but he could not hear them.

He started to cry out to Betty Sheldon, but he knew that that would prove her undoing. He could only keep silent and hope. He was unable to get back on the Wall, and unless he moved swiftly they would be upon him and he would be unable to help her or anyone else ever again.

Scrambling over the rough stone-clad hill, he found a cleft

· L. RON HUBBARD ·

under a rock. His fingers tore at the harsh dirt. He was sick in both heart and body for the first time in years. Those devils would get Betty Sheldon, and he could do nothing about it. He had to rest on his oars and hope for the best.

The hole he dug was large enough for him to crawl into. He was sheltered, then, from the blasting fire above him and from eyes in the dark. Raking up dirt, he covered half of his body and lay still, waiting. It was not until then that he realized how badly he had been shaken up in the fall.

The letdown came over him like a straitjacket. He felt unable to move his shoulders, and his chest burned as though someone were stabbing him with a hot iron. His back muscles had been severely wrenched by the fall, and his right ankle had begun to swell inside his artillery boot. By moving his arm he was able to feel the boot and knew that he would not be able to remove it unless he cut the leather with his knife.

He didn't think the soldiers and Blakely would go away from there without at least searching for his body, which would be worth a hundred thousand yen to the Japanese alone, and he was right.

A half-hour dragged itself away before he heard footsteps. By looking through the slanting hole he had left for vision, he could see the circle of lantern light approaching on the ground. Legs swung great shadows across the arc. A man was muttering unintelligibly.

Stuart thanked his guiding stars that rain was a foreign thing to this terrain. Otherwise his digging would have left a damp patch of dark ground. As it was, there was little trace in the sandy soil.

The lantern came nearer. Stuart braced himself on one elbow and slipped a clip into the one automatic that remained to him. A shot would call them all down upon him, but he would at least make a try at escape.

Watching the yellow circle swing in toward the rock, he was more concerned about Betty Sheldon than he was about himself. He had played at this game of chance so long that his nerves were dulled where danger was concerned, but Betty Sheldon was alive to every smallest detail. In spite of her trips with her father, she remained sensitive to even minor danger. It had no effect whatever on her courage, but it was hard on her nerves.

Stuart was assailed by the agonizing thought that he was really responsible for her presence here. He had offered his help. He had made these plans. Perhaps if he had refused she would have given up.

But he knew that he was wrong in that. Betty Sheldon was not a girl who would give up so easily. And besides, she had been dead broke, unable even to pay her hotel bill, though she had never said anything about it until he found her out. And she would not have accepted money from him if he had not taken her with him. And above and beyond all that, she wanted to realize her father's dream and find the Black Chest, which lay around somewhere in Manchuria.

The circle of light was almost under the rock. If the man who held the lantern stooped two feet lower, he would be able to see Stuart's shoulder.

Stuart realized in that instant that he once more had a purpose in living. He had to live long enough to get Betty

Sheldon out of this mess. After that he could see to it that she had enough money to leave the country. He himself would never be able to leave. The seaports and steamship offices were too well posted for that. They had his picture displayed before every ticket counter all the way down the China coast. He had tried stowing away once, but he had only escaped by the width of a hair.

No, he would play this hand to the finish, get Betty Sheldon out of the country, and then take the death which fate had been dangling before him these last long months, when the game had lost its tang.

The man with the light stooped and stared under the rock. Without moving, Stuart drew his sights on the man's face. By lantern light he could see the midnight hue of the eyes. As soon as the mouth opened to shout a warning, Stuart would blast the man into oblivion.

The circle of yellow light swung uneasily as the lantern was buffeted by the wind. The soldier lifted it up, trying to see a little better. Stuart's finger tightened on the steel. In an instant he would fire the shot which would give him away, but which could not be avoided.

But the shot remained in the gun, to serve a later purpose. The soldier straightened up and moved away to stare under other boulders.

Stuart sighed with relief. Cold sweat was standing out against his forehead. He knew what had happened, why the man had gazed so long. The soldier was blinded by his own lantern. Had he carried a flashlight, it would have been an entirely different story. Grimed of face, Stuart had offered but a small patch of white to view—enough to be mistaken for a patch of green fungus under a boulder.

Other footsteps passed by, voices came near and then departed, and as the night progressed toward morning Stuart was stiff with cold and shaking with the nervous strain. He had heard no cry of victory up there on the Wall. He hoped, fiercely, that they hadn't found Betty Sheldon, even though he knew that missing her along the Wall would be an impossibility.

The cloudiness of the coming day obscured the dawn and it was seven in the morning by Stuart's wristwatch when the first shafts of light struck the bleak, sharp hillsides.

He had heard no sounds for an hour and he crawled cautiously forth, trying not to hurt his ankle. He knew that he would need it badly.

No one was in sight. Evidently they had gone, thinking that he had made good his escape. Assured of the fact, Stuart stood up and limped toward the base of the Wall. He was on the China side, he noted with relief. Perhaps he could find a postern in daylight and climb up on the Wall again.

However, that was not necessary. The rope ladder the sentry had lowered in the darkness still dangled from an embrasure. Racked and weary, Stuart mounted up, using only one foot. He stopped at the top, unwilling to go over the edge before he had made sure he was alone.

After a slow scrutiny he felt satisfied and managed to crawl through the notch in the stone. He inched forward on his knees, until he could see around the bend.

Instantly he froze. Not twenty feet from him, a red-tabbed officer was leaning against the battlement, looking in the other direction, smoking a cigarette. If he turned and saw Stuart in that moment, Stuart knew that he would be unable to draw in time to save himself. He was too tired, too bruised. If it had not been for Betty Sheldon, he would not have cared.

The yellow face jerked around. Some slight movement of Stuart's had caught the slanted eyes. A swarthy hand darted down to the tan holster. Stuart had been unwilling to shoot. He knew that there must be others in this man's patrol, and a shot would call them all down upon him. But there was no way out of it now. The swarthy hand came up with a stubby gun.

Stuart drew and fired in the same instant. A third eye came into being in the Japanese forehead. Without a sound, the man slumped. Stuart's boots raced over the even pavement. He forgot that he was tired and bruised. He forgot everything but the job at hand and the fact that he had not yet seen Betty Sheldon.

A shout came up from the north side of the Wall. Three cavalrymen were there, dismounting, running toward the rope ladders, which swung in the wind.

From the crest of the hill a Japanese soldier sprinted down, rifle carried at port. From the east swarmed a swirling mass of mustard cloth and red insignia. The cry, *"Akai Tatsu!* The Red Dragon!"* was shrill in the morning air.

A second officer gained the rampart, revolver in hand. He was breathing heavily from his struggle up the face of the Wall, but his eyes were beady with the thought of one hundred thousand yen.

Two hundred feet from this officer, a mustard-uniformed man with the bars of captain waved his gun down at the China side.

"Acki! Akai Tatsu!" howled the man with captain's bars.

The newcomer shot a glance out across the hills. The captain's voice was insistent. The cavalrymen were less hard to convince. When they gained the top they slid off the other side immediately, to run in the direction the captain was pointing out. The infantryman and the others dropped over the China side in full cry, like a pack of beagle hounds in sight of the fox.

When they had gone, the man with captain's bars turned down the collar of his coat and displayed the face of Michael Stuart. He scanned the surface of the pavement. A small, crumpled bit of paper was skidding toward him, borne on the wind, as though begging to be picked up.

Stuart glanced at it and unfolded it. It was only a slip made black by the uneven splotch of pencil marks. He was about to throw it aside and make good his escape when he saw that the pencil marks had been made while the paper was held on an uneven surface. It was an old trick, known to all school children. Betty Sheldon had placed this paper over the back of the locket and transmitted to it the scratching which lay in the gold.

Stuart knew, then, that he held the chart that would lead to the Black Chest.

He looked up toward Manchuria, his face taut. Then his eyes turned toward the west where Betty Sheldon must have been taken. He had never fully realized the faith she must have in him. If she had believed everything that had been told her about the Red Dragon, she would not have dared place the secret so fully in his hands. Hadn't she known how easy it would be for him to go off and leave her?

Stuart turned up his coat collar again and headed for a rope ladder which would lead into Jehol. His mind was busy with plans of rescue and he did not let himself dwell on the possibility of Betty Sheldon's death.

Glancing back at a depression in the pavement, he made certain that the Japanese officer's body would not be easily discovered. Then he swung down the sheer face of the masonry and ran toward one of the cavalry horses. Mounting, he dug in his spurs and galloped west.

The cries of the searching Japanese were lost in the silence of the Western Hills.

Chapter Six

TRACKS in sand are impermanent things. The small wind covers them inches deep. Sometimes an experienced woodsman can trail through underbrush merely by watching for broken twigs and reeds, but here in this barren waste there were no shrubs. Only hard rock and shifting, dry dirt.

For the past week Michael Stuart, the Red Dragon, had depended utterly upon the unreliable memories of the Chinese immigrants who were busy trying to farm this unfarmable country.

Yes, they saw many bodies of Japanese troops. Yes, some of them were going north. No, there hadn't been any white people in the party. Oh, yes, there had been two or three supply carts in some of the detachments and these, of course, might carry white people. One never knew just what the Japanese did, begging the Japanese officer's pardon.

Occasionally the black eyes of the Chinese widened with surprise. But few Japanese officers could even attempt to speak the south-of-the-Wall dialects. However, they knew nothing of Japanese affairs. Since the short ones with bristly hair had come to this part of the north, the immigrants had only hoped that they would find the taxes fair and the troops not too demanding. Of course, the bandits were much worse of late. The armies, you see, had disbanded, and the Chinese

61

soldiers had taken up the only trade they knew, even though that trade was suddenly illegal.

No, they couldn't remember having seen a white girl.

Michael Stuart rode on, pushing ever north. At first he had searched along the Wall, but he knew that Blakely wouldn't stay there when the Red Dragon was still on the loose. Blakely would now be in possession of the golden locket. If Betty Sheldon lived up to her standards of past resourcefulness, then she would have given Blakely the locket and would even be aiding him in the search for the Black Chest, whatever it contained.

She might have been told that the Red Dragon was dead, and in that case she would act differently. Stuart reasoned that she had been told that, and that she would probably refuse to believe it until the body was located and shown to her.

A little yellow dirt had colored Stuart's face well enough and a little adhesive tape from the first-aid kit in his hip pocket had served to give his eyes the proper slant. The color of his eyes was his only concern, and he wore his Japanese cap low and always sat with his back to the sun or light when talking to people.

The cavalry horse had been equipped with a compass and map of the entire Japanese conquest, and by comparing these with the faint smudge map Betty had left him, Stuart hoped that he was making fair progress in the direction of the cache.

He was puzzled about one thing in particular. He had not asked Betty for a complete description of the ground. Would the Black Chest lay in a forgotten city? The marks on the chart seemed to indicate that. Perhaps he would better understand those notations when he came to the site of the river which joined a circle that might be a lake.

On the evening of the seventh day, Stuart cantered into the village of Bekiri, alert for the presence of Japanese soldiers, and on the watch for an eating house.

The village was nothing more than a series of mud and straw huts along one side of a railroad track. This, the southeastern boundary of the Gobi or Shamo Desert, was hemmed in by treeless, sandy wastes, where, with the aid of field glasses, a horseman could be seen for thirty miles. It was not an encouraging country for a fugitive, but Stuart was bluffing out his disguise.

One hut was a little longer than the rest and from the center of the roof smoke was pouring out, to drag along the ground. A grizzled Manchurian sat before the door, smoking an opium pipe and watching the evening crowd of a dozen people promenade.

Stuart spoke to the ancient one, gruffly. "I require a bed and food, and quarters for my horse."

The ancient one looked up and bobbed his scraggly beard. "The Japanese barracks, Captain, are but a mile to the north."

"*Burei naru saru!* Insolent ape! Is that a proper manner with which to treat an officer of the Mikado? I shall order the village burned and the people slaughtered."

The ancient one shrugged and called softly back through the doorway. He had the air of one who has borne much, but who expects no other lot. A boy came out and took Stuart's horse.

Slipping a silver piece into the boy's hand, Stuart said, "Rub him down thoroughly, and then resaddle him and say nothing."

The boy eyed the money, bit it with yellow teeth, and then shoved it deep in his padded jacket. He nodded vigorously and watched Stuart bow his head to enter the door.

The interior of the hut was filled with rolling smoke which stung the eyes. The makeshift chimney did not draw well in the quiet air. Manchurians sat against the walls, feet drawn up under them. They either smoked and talked, or thrust a watery porridge into their drooling mouths, as though they did not expect to eat again for months to come. Two less shabbily dressed men—obviously men about town—sat aloof from the rest and sipped tea.

Stuart, as befitting the station his bars gave him, sat down away from the rest and imperiously ordered an impossible menu which included three kinds of fowl, roast pork and rice. By doing this he was assured that he would at least receive something more than porridge. The woman who waited upon him brought him a small table and a cushion, and a glass of hot red sake.

Sipping at the rice liquor, Stuart looked closely at the crowd. They would not be able to see the color of his eyes through this smoke because he had placed himself just under a pot of oil and a wick, which served as a lantern.

One of the men-about-town glanced in Stuart's direction and then looked back, more intently. Stuart dropped his eyes and stared into the red liquor, thinking. There was something familiar about that man's face, even though it was made up, obviously, with grease paint and black pencil.

Stuart stared at the man and then set down the glass. It was Jigoku Neko, the Hell-Cat. Stuart had thought that he might meet the man, because Suga, the Hell-Cat, was everywhere, spying on everyone, always on the lookout for possible danger to the Mikado's troops. And Suga, of course, would be following in Blakely's wake or, more likely, acting as Blakely's vanguard. A fleeting thought made Stuart wonder why Blakely was suddenly so thick with the Japanese.

Another thought jolted Stuart. If he, Stuart, could recognize Jigoku Neko, then why couldn't Jigoku Neko recognize him?

Suga, the Hell-Cat, got to his feet and, teacup in hand, made his way around legs and small foot-high tables until he came to Stuart's side.

"*Oyasumi nasare!* Good evening," said Suga, smiling.

Stuart did not know whether he ought to shoot Suga immediately or trust his brand of Japanese. He decided that, with a Japanese barracks a mile away, peace would be more in order.

Accordingly, he answered, "*Oyasumi nasare,* Suga Jigoku Neko."

The Hell-Cat started, and spilled some of his tea on Stuart's table.

"You have heard of me? You recognize me? Speak lower. I do not want these people to hear." He squatted down on his haunches, bringing his face lower than Stuart's. He could not see clearly due to the light which shone in his eyes.

"Who," breathed Stuart, "has not heard of the mighty exploits of the Honorable Suga Jigoku Neko? And who has not seen his pictures in the Tokyo press?"

"Taichō! Watakushi wa odoroku iru!" whispered Suga. "Captain! I am amazed!"

"You are modest," countered Stuart. "How are things in Manchuria?"

"You should know better than I."

"Not I. I have just returned, Honorable Suga, from Inner Mongolia, and I hunger for news of General Shimokado's exploits. I will not be able to join his command immediately, as—"

"Go on," begged Suga, thirsting for information himself.

"It happens that I cannot disclose my mission as it is of great secrecy. I trust the Honorable Suga will understand, as he too is a man of great missions."

"Thoroughly," said Suga, throwing out his thick chest and setting down his tea. "You would be amazed at the mission that now calls my attention. I have worthy word that the devil known as the Red Dragon is in this country, and I search the highways in disguise for word of him."

"A perilous mission. Were your fame less great, they should send out a regiment."

Suga smiled. "They have patrols combing every gully from here to the Wall. We will get him this time, of that I am sure. And his death will not be sweet. But first his agony shall be raised to such a monstrous pitch that he will break down and tell us where he keeps Shimokado's brother. Then we will kill him, slowly, slowly. I myself will watch it."

"A perilous mission," agreed Stuart. "But they have chosen a worthy man to handle it. I wish that I could have so great a task. The man who receives the body of the Red Dragon will be famous forever."

"And rich," said Suga excitedly. "The folly of Shimokado! He keeps face by offering a hundred thousand yen reward for the body of the Red Dragon. It is said that he even carries it with him wherever he goes, so that he can pay off quickly. The knowledge is destined to stimulate a speedy death of the Red Dragon, *taichō*. Shimokado's face still burns with the knowledge that his brother was captured with such great ease—and out of the office of General Headquarters, too."

Stuart nodded. "But what can bring the Red Dragon back to Manchuria?"

"Ah!" breathed Suga. "There are none that know besides myself and a handful of soldiers."

"Of course. I expected that a man of such great sight as yourself would know."

"Certainly I know. I know all things. It is my trade."

"But of course you could not be expected to know every detail of it."

Suga Jigoku Neko bristled with importance. "And why, may I ask, do you think that I do not know every detail?"

"No one could possibly know the plans of the Red Dragon."

"No?" cried Suga. "No? Then listen. He is here in Manchuria, tracing a party of soldiers into the north country. This *Akai Tatsu* has the nose of a Siberian wolf. He can scent their tracks in the dust. Each night he watches them from afar, and then rides away like the wind, so that they cannot catch him."

Stuart's heart drummed on his ribs. This meant that he could not be far from Betty Sheldon and Blakely.

"But why should he follow them?"

"Because," breathed Suga, "in that party is a captive, the girl he loves. He wishes to rescue her so that they can recover the Black Chest, which is filled with riches, and then flee back to China."

"But why are they taking the girl to the north? Why don't they take her to General Headquarters and send out the news for bait?"

"Because these soldiers and a white man named Blakely are also searching for the Black Chest. They have taken a locket from the girl which bears the map of the region and the directions for locating this Black Chest. After they have found that, they will take the girl to Headquarters as you suggest, and the Red Dragon will, of course, give himself up, in the hope that she will go free. Of course," smiled Suga, "we will kill both of them then. We want no foreign powers to raise a cry about the matter."

"Blakely," said Stuart. "Perhaps I have heard of him."

"Certainly you have. He is our spy in Peking. For years he has been on the trail of the Black Chest, as a sideline. Now he is willing to split half and half with the Mikado, and we have given him every aid."

"Certainly it has been said that you are wise," said Stuart. His food had been brought to him and he welcomed the opportunity of lowering his eyes. Any change in the lamp above would immediately reveal the fact that his eyes were steel gray instead of black. And with a murderer sitting before him and a barracks of troops a mile away, Stuart was apprehensive.

"I am wiser than wise," chuckled Suga, bloated with flattery. "I know that they have already found the Black Chest and are even now heading for Harbin."

The news was startling. Stuart shot out the question as though it were a bullet. "Are you sure of that?"

Instantly, Suga deflated to a well-oiled, efficient spy machine. "You are too interested," he rasped, and a small automatic appeared in his left hand.

"Of course I am interested," said Stuart, continuing to eat. "I am always interested in the exploits of so great a man as Suga Jigoku Neko."

"Turn around and face the light," ordered Suga in a deadly voice. "I have a feeling that I know you."

Stuart shrugged and started to turn. Like a bolt of lightning, the table catapulted up into Suga's face. Suga screamed and whipped down with the gun.

Stuart's holster flap quivered. The lamp glinted on blued steel. The room was hacked apart by the blinding flash of exploding powder.

Suga, a bundle of dirty cloth, sagged back against a supporting pole. Particles of splattered food mixed with the blood on his face.

The automatic swept the room. "Quiet!" snapped Stuart. "This man was a spy from China. I have killed him. Leave him where he lies until I return from the barracks with troops!"

"Quiet!" snapped Stuart. "This man was a spy from China. I have killed him."

The man with whom Suga had been speaking moved restlessly. In the next second Stuart knew they had seen his eyes, his gray eyes. The knowledge was like a shower of ice water. The man who had moved, moved again. Stuart fired before the other's gun was halfway leveled. The man's weapon rapped a shot into the dirt floor. The plowed hole was immediately covered by his body.

Stuart raced for the back of the hut. He stumbled against a boy and saw that the horse was just beyond, saddled and ready to go. He vaulted into the saddle and the spurred pony reared twice before it shot away toward the north.

Turning down a ravine, Stuart headed west and then south. When he was well out of sight, he again headed west. His pony's hoofs rolled like miniature kettledrums against the hard sand.

Chapter Seven

MICHAEL STUART dismounted with a shiver. The country was cold just before dawn, bitterly cold, and the wind cut through the regulation Japanese officer's overcoat as though it had been constructed of cheesecloth. Stuart thought to himself, as he climbed the knifelike ridge on foot, that the Japanese quartermaster corps might have been more thoughtful.

From Stuart's shoulder swung a pair of field glasses he had appropriated with the horse. They were mostly tin, and their lenses were faulty, but they served their purpose well enough. The Japanese, thought Stuart, as he adjusted the setscrew, could hardly be expected to manufacture German-quality glass.

A small cloud of dust was rising in the east and, knowing that he was visible against the skyline, he stretched his length on the near side of the ridge and braced his elbows. He scrutinized the cloud and saw horses at the bottom of it. Evidently the party was coming toward him.

Something sparkled in the dust and then flashed again. For an instant the wind took the cloud away and then dropped it back like a curtain. The instant had been sufficient. This was a band of Japanese cavalry and, judging by their formation, they were on the scout for something or someone. Stuart knew their objective, then. They were searching for the man who had killed Suga Jigoku Neko the night before, and they knew that man to be the Red Dragon.

Stuart turned around and examined the terrain to the south. Another cloud of dust was there, and another patrol. Wheeling again, he saw a flash of something in the north and played the glasses over it. But the flash did not come from pennoned lances in the cold morning sun. It was a body of water, a lake of large dimensions.

He knew that he had the choice of two objectives. He could head for the lake and perhaps be trapped against the water, or he could head due west and take his chances with the patrol coming up from the south. East and south were blocked. Cocking the military cap over his eye, Stuart hoped that he'd live long enough to find Betty Sheldon and get her away. After that, what happened wouldn't matter so much. He couldn't leave the country anyway, and he was certainly far from in love with it.

Lying there on the edge of the ridge, he remembered a row of oak trees along a quiet street banked by white-columned houses. There was a drugstore at the far end where you could buy a soda to quench your thirst, and there was a movie theater across from the drugstore where you could have two hours' amusement for two bits. The usher sometimes let kids in when he thought the manager wasn't looking. Beside the movie theater was a store porch where the oldtimers sat and talked about the good old days and what ought to be done about the government. In the store you ate crackers and pickles while your order was being filled or while the storekeeper congratulated

Mrs. Brown upon her daughter's new baby. You could lie under those trees and sleep for hours, with nothing to—

Stuart jolted himself up into a sitting position and half slid, half ran down the hill to his pony. The east patrol was getting too close for comfort.

The jaded horse looked back at his rider, a reproachful look in his usually vicious eyes. Then he set his hammer head toward the bottom of the gully and scrambled along, too weary to pick up his feet.

Having crossed a low range of hills in the night, Stuart found that the country was leveling out toward the lake. The ground was less hard, even damp in places. Looking back, he saw that his horse was leaving well-defined prints. All the damp ground was in the depressions, and he could not leave them for the open plains. There was no way to avoid leaving prints, if he wanted to remain out of sight.

Stuart knew that they would pick up his trail sometime that day. He would have to work fast and strike fast to get out from under the executioner's ax. They would not be watching for a white man now, but for a Japanese officer with gray eyes.

Picking his way carefully, Stuart found himself on a flat surface, a washed-out canyon floor. He reined in and studied the side wall. A campfire had been there and its smoke had blackened the rock above it.

He climbed down and approached it. There were numerous tracks about the place. Many of them showed the big toe to be separated from the main part of the foot. That would mean Japanese split-toed sandals, of the type soldiers wore.

A small spring was nearby and Stuart looked at the tracks around it, where the mud had held them better defined.

The first discovery he made was the impression of a European shoe. The next was that of a boot print, too small for any man. Betty Sheldon's!

Weariness dropped from him like a discarded cloak. Blakely and Betty had been along here, and they had left a trail toward the lake. Stuart studied the map Betty had left him. The circle, then, *was* a lake. And the other marks must mean a series of caves, not houses.

He mounted and spurred his pony into a trot. This site was undoubtedly their last camp before they reached the lake. And, wanting sunlight for the search, they had undoubtedly stopped near enough to make the site in an hour's march the following morning. The fact amused Stuart a little. They had been afraid to go near the caves in the dark, had been afraid of *Akai Tatsu*, the Red Dragon.

Because he was alone, unimpeded by numbers and baggage, Stuart made the distance in something less than an hour. He saw the lake first, a limitless expanse of blue, refreshing after days of tan desert.

Approaching the water, he looked back, and saw a line of holes on a cliffside above him. From where he stood, they were no larger than bullet marks in mud, but a glance with the field glasses showed that they were of considerable diameter.

Stuart hid his pony in a clump of trees. It had grown warmer and he shed his overcoat before he started the climb. He made certain that both his guns were ready for action in case they had an ambush planned for him.

The first hill was gradual, but after that the side shot up—almost perpendicular. Evidently Blakely had not liked the climb, for the soldiers had cut small steps out of the dirt, and the ascent was not too difficult.

Fifteen minutes of steady work brought Stuart to the first cave. He studied the chart and decided that this was not the one. From cave to cave he made his way, peering into the musty darkness.

He consulted the chart again, checked his count, and then entered an open maw confidently. A shaft of sunlight swept in, lighting his way. It glittered on something which looked like a spider web.

It was a copper wire, strung at the height of a man's waist. It was invisible in darkness, and in another hour the sun would have been too high to have shown it up.

Following its length without touching it, Stuart traced it to one wall. He looked into a small hole which was freshly dug. He reached inside, gingerly, and pulled out a black object—a hand grenade.

This, then, was a murder trap of the first degree. If he had walked into the wire, the hand grenade's ring would have been pulled out and he would either have been killed outright or entombed under tons of debris.

He battened down the ring and slid the grenade into his hip pocket. It was not dangerous when locked, and they had thoughtfully left the locking pin attached to it. That Blakely would stoop to such tactics angered Stuart. To shoot a man was one thing, but to set a bomb deliberately was quite another. Blakely had one more score to pay up.

77

Beyond the wire lay a series of galleries in the walls. Stuart glanced in the first, then recoiled. He had not expected to see a scattered pile of human bones, topped by a grinning skull. The eyes stared at him unwinking as though accusing him of desecration. And desecration had been done. The framework of a man had lain here for centuries, preserved by red ochre paint. Only recently had it been disturbed. Within the last twenty-four hours.

Stuart went down the passageway, groping through the dark, not knowing what he would find. His hands touched the edge of a box and he yanked it toward him. It did not come easily and he lit a match to find out why.

The box was made from imperishable iron wood from some far-off tropical country. It had lain in this cave for hundreds of years. Its weight had carried it down into the flinty dirt of the floor.

But the box contained no riches. Only the red ochre painted skeleton of a man who must have been seven feet tall. The bones were pulled apart, as though in anger.

The Black Chest, then, was nothing more than a coffin which might have contained a king. In itself, it was valueless. Stuart felt let down. There might have been something here, but it was gone now. Perhaps Blakely and his troops had taken it, but whatever it was, it could not have been very large.

Stuart retraced his steps to the front of the cave and then made his way down the hillside to his horse.

He was upset, somehow. He was thinking of the tortures Betty Sheldon must have had to bear. That is, if she thought anything of him at all. She had watched them erect that murder trap up there, and she would think that he was dead by this time.

He found the trail left by Blakely and his men. It headed east, almost into the arms of the patrol, which still raised a cloud of dust across the plain. Stuart counted the number of hoofs in the trail and decided that Blakely must have about eight men with him. Certainly no more than that.

Once more he thought of the fate that lay ahead of him, but he also thought of the way he had brought Betty Sheldon into all this. It was his fault that she was here, and he had to get her out of it—if he could.

He spurred into the east, keeping below the ridges, picking up Blakely's trail at intervals. They had evidently searched long up there in the caves, as they had made another camp only two hours' ride to the east. Stuart passed it at a trot, satisfied that Betty Sheldon was still with them.

The sun grew warmer and down in the gullies it was stifling. Stuart paused long enough to shed his coat and roll up his sleeves. There was little use keeping up the pretense of being a Japanese officer. They all knew his disguise by this time, and besides, he was tired of having his eyes drawn back. He stopped again beside a brook and washed his face of the brown dirt.

As he sat back in the saddle, the grenade was against the crosstrees. It made him uncomfortable, for the safety pin might come out. Looking for a place to put the bomb, he decided upon his bulky sleeve. When he pinned the cuff tight, the grenade was not too bunglesome. It weighed but little, to pack such a terrific punch.

At two o'clock, Stuart stopped again. He fished a soggy cracker out of his saddlebag and ate, watching from a ridge. He was flanking the patrol by now, less than a mile away from it. If they had spread out any scouts, Stuart reasoned that he could expect trouble in large quantities.

To the east lay a pass between two low buttes. Beyond it, lined up like the sights of a gun, was another pass. Training the field glasses through the first notch, Stuart sighted the third cloud of dust he had seen that day. The brown, swirling blob was too far away to be distinct, but he was certain it contained horsemen.

Hastily he climbed up to a higher pinnacle and swept the south. The patrol he had sighted that morning was heading toward the notch. The second patrol was only three gullies away from him, also heading east. In the last patrol there was a full troop of cavalry, moving slowly and sweeping all the country to the right and left.

Stuart knew the answer to that. All patrols were heading east. Something must lay in the second notch. This nearby group had changed their course for only one reason, it was clear. They had found Stuart's trail.

Sliding and scrambling, Stuart went back to his horse. Only one course remained to him. They were coming up behind like a dragnet. They had him cut off to the south. He would be trapped against the lake if he went north. He could go in only one direction—straight ahead toward the two passes—thereby running the risk of being sighted while crossing the plain.

Even as he counted the odds against him if he went out into the open, he found himself at the gully's end, confronting a barren, level strip of land. He could not remain where he was, but as soon as the nearby squadrons sighted him out there, the end would be in sight. And far, far ahead was another cloud of dust, beyond the first notch.

Always a gambler, Stuart took the chance. His pony had had some slight rest and he might be able to make the dash. It was less than three miles to the first pass. If he could get through that, he might be able to avoid the troop beyond and get through the second. Betty Sheldon was within ten miles of where he rode, of that he was certain.

Spurring the horse and laying on with the loose rein ends, he rocketed out into the open. He hovered low in the saddle for the first thousand yards, expecting shots from the rear. After that he was out of rifle range, until he went through the first notch.

Riding across the flat expanse made him feel like a mechanical duck in a shooting gallery. From three sides they were only waiting for an opportunity to pot him. He would find no quarter here.

He reined in for a moment, looking back. He was two-thirds of the way across, and still no sign of the Japanese on the knolls behind him. A flash of sun on metal would tell him. Thank heaven the Japanese went in for fancy ornaments on their soldier suits!

He was off again. The sheer sides of the buttes directly before him rose with each advancing foot while, in direct contrast, the second notch, visible through the first, seemed to recede.

The pony's hoofs clattered on harder surface as he went through. It was like a gate in a high board fence, thought Stuart, with the exception that there was no gate.

With a sigh of relief he saw that the patrol ahead was going in the same direction he was. Maybe he could get around them. If he could locate Blakely's party, he could at least make a stab at—

Abruptly two mustard-colored soldiers leaped out from rocks ahead of him, rifles to shoulder. Stuart jerked to a stop and started to wheel, in the hope that he could run for it. But on the wall above his head two more soldiers jumped up, like Punch and Judy.

"Walked right into it, didn't you, Red Dragon! Right into the trap! Dismount, and throw your guns on the ground!"

Stuart's cold eyes rested on the face of Blakely for a full minute. Blakely shifted uneasily. Stuart stepped down and unholstered his weapons, which he dropped on the sand. From somewhere near he heard Betty Sheldon cry out, "Mike! Oh, Mike! I thought you were dead!"

Chapter Eight

THEY had tied the Red Dragon securely, with his back to a rock. George Blakely, looking like a vulture in black riding clothes, stepped back, and craned his neck at Stuart.

"Now that that's done," he said in a raucous voice, "I'd better signal the patrols that I've got you."

"Going to turn me over to them alive, eh?" said Stuart.

"Certainly—let them have their fun. You've caused them enough trouble, and they've earned a little sport."

"I'm sure they have," Stuart replied. He looked over toward the rock where Betty Sheldon sat.

She was white of face, and her deep blue eyes were almost black with anxiety. Her clothing, which had been so trim in Peking, was now in rags. Her boots were scuffed beyond all possibility of shining them again, and her jacket was now a collection of triangular rips.

"What are you going to do with her?" said Stuart.

"Well, just to make you feel good, Red Dragon, let me inform you that she will be taken to Harbin and turned over to the Japanese authorities. Whatever they wish to do with her, they can."

"And you call yourself a respectable man!" said Stuart.

Blakely's laugh was unpleasant. "Trying to appeal to my

honor, that it? Well, I know I haven't any use for a woman, and I'm certainly not going to let her run around the country getting me into trouble. But why worry yourself about these things? You have just about twenty-four hours to live. Maybe not that."

"Why?"

"Because I sent a message to General Shimokado that I expected to trap you today one way or another, and he promised to come before sundown. He will undoubtedly shoot you on sight, and you should be thankful. These Japanese can think of some unpleasant things to do to a man."

"And how did you send this message?" asked Stuart.

"What difference does that make to you? But, then, I'd better humor a dead man. I sent it by heliograph as soon as the sun came up this morning, and the troops that have quarters on the next range relayed it. I know my way around."

"Pretty clever. Then none of these men have ever been away from you, have they?"

"Of course not!" cried Blakely, irritably.

"Thanks," said the Red Dragon, smiling with cold eyes. "You'd better be sending that signal and tell the squadrons that you've got me and they better close in."

"Who's running your execution, anyway?" Blakely demanded. Picking up the mirror, shutter, and sight which made up the heliographing set, he climbed up to the butte top some three hundred yards away.

Two Japanese soldiers sat near Stuart, rifles on their knees, eyes beady and watchful. As soon as Blakely was out of sight, one of them found a cigarette and lit it.

Stuart sighed and looked at Betty. She came over to him, trying to be calm.

"What happened to the Black Chest?" Stuart asked.

"It was a terrible disappointment," she said, her voice almost level. "See those burlap bags over there? They contain some rock carvings, that's all. They're beautifully done, but they are worth nothing. I suppose my dad was just after them because they could trace some era of culture."

"What color are they?" asked Stuart.

"Dark brown, all of them. They aren't any good. That's why Blakely is so vindictive toward you and me. We led him through all this rough country and he found nothing. He means now to collect your . . . your—"

"Blood money," supplied Stuart. And then in the same conversational tone, he said, "These soldiers do not speak English." He looked at them quietly, but neither so much as blinked. "Look, Betty. They have tied my right wrist with a square knot. If it is a little loose, it immediately becomes a pair of half hitches. Pretend that you are all broken up about my being caught and grab my arm. Loosen that knot, understand?"

"Oh, Mike!" she cried, obediently emotional, and grabbed his right wrist with both slim hands. Under the cover of her palms, she pulled at the knot.

One of the soldiers jumped up, jerked her away from Stuart, and sent her reeling against the stone side of the pit.

"Don't try to get loose," said Betty, in a hopeless voice. "They've got us both now. I can't stay in China, and you will never be able to leave. It isn't any use. We might as well—"

"Hush," said Stuart, smiling.

"But there are six other soldiers around here," she protested. "Four of them are up there with Blakely, helping him signal. The other two are down below us in the pass, watching the cavalry come up."

"Stand up on that rock," Stuart ordered. "Is there anything coming toward us from the east?"

She did his bidding. "Yes. It's an entire company, and they're starting to come in from the west and south. We can't get away, even if you get loose." She sat down on the rock, facing him across the pit. "They'll all be here in fifteen minutes. There isn't time for anything!"

"These soldiers are not looking at you," said Stuart. "Stand up and point at the pass, and look happy about it." He changed to Japanese. "Things will not go so easily, *tsuwamono*, when my own troops arrive."

The two stared at one another. Betty sprang up and pointed down to the pass. Involuntarily the two Japanese darted to their feet and jumped up on the rim.

Stuart twisted his right wrist. The rope slipped into two half hitches and came off in an instant. He yanked at the knots of his left and pulled it free. He ripped at the laces of his boots and yanked them off.

Before the soldiers could turn, Stuart sprang at the feet of the first and pulled him down. The Japanese hit the rock floor with his head and lay still. The other whirled, his blue brown jowls slack.

Stuart dived for the rifle of the first. Out of the corner of his eye he saw the blue brown jowls quiver over gunsights.

86

The shot, hastily put, buried itself at Stuart's feet. The flame singed his hair.

It took the soldier an instant to jack another shell into the chamber. Stuart raised the dead man's gun to his hip and pulled the trigger. The blue brown jowls went slack. Doubled up, the Japanese came off the rock rim like a high diver in a jackknife.

Stuart turned to face the ridge, pulling Betty into cover. "I guess we're trapped," he said. "We can't move as long as they are there, and the squadrons will be up in the space of ten minutes."

Crouching beside him, she looked up into his face. He knew that she depended upon him utterly—more than that, she loved him. Something round and heavy joggled in Stuart's sleeve.

He took the black object out, staring at it. Suddenly he grinned and juggled the hand grenade.

From the pit to the rock which hid Blakely and the rest of his forces it was less than fifty yards. But even that was too far. Half a city block is quite a distance to pitch a hand grenade.

Slipping over the edge, Stuart motioned Betty to stay down. Sliding the rifle ahead of him, he wormed his way across the flat toward the rock, watching for any movement there. Down the pass he could see the first squadron arriving.

At a distance of fifty feet, Stuart pulled the pin out of the grenade, pulled the metal that would start the fuse. He counted, "One! Two! Three!"—mustn't get rid of it too soon, they might throw it back at him. "Four!"

With an overhand motion he sent the grenade soaring through the air. Five feet above the boulder it burst. Shrapnel sang over Stuart's head and ricocheted off stone.

A man screamed on the other side. Abruptly a man rose up, flinging his arms over his head. Stuart was unable to believe his eyes. It was Blakely, unscathed.

Blakely saw Stuart in the same instant. He tried to duck again, but before he did, he sent a revolver shot point-blank at Stuart. Stuart did not sight the rifle, but he knew where the bullet would go. Knew just where it would strike Blakely. Knew just how low to aim to hit that moving mark. Knew just why Blakely had to be shot in that place.

Blakely's arms went up like a scarecrow's. He flopped, feebly, kicked his scrawny legs. His twitching hands found a stone and clung to it. Then his head jutted out into Stuart's sight. The man who had been George Blakely no longer had a face.

Stuart made certain that the two other Japanese were dead. Betty started toward him, but he waved her back, his face strained. "Get the frying pans from their baggage. Quickly!"

She ran down toward a small ridge and returned in a few moments with the strange articles. She stopped beside the pit, her mouth dropping open with amazement.

Stuart was now dressed in Blakely's clothes. And in the center of a pit, ringed by empty cartridges, was a bloody thing, scarcely recognizable as the former George Blakely. The body was dressed in the clothing Stuart had worn.

Stuart offered no explanations. He yanked the frying pans out of her hands and scraped off black smudge from the bottoms. When he had a small pile of it, he rubbed it into his hair, into his eyebrows. Pouring water from a canteen, he rid his fingers of the black, greasy substance.

That done, Stuart pulled at the bodies in the pit and threw them outside, climbing up to drag them behind rocks. Slightly sick at the sight of this carnage, Betty stood by, white of face.

"You mean you'll try to be Blakely?" she gasped.

"Yes. I don't know whether or not these others have seen him. Blakely operated in North China and Jehol, and this is a different region, and under a different staff. If I can pass myself off for him, we can get away."

Hoofs were pounding in the pass and the dust rolled up like a brown thundercloud. Stuart walked down the incline, waiting.

The first man to dismount was an officer. He paid little attention to Stuart. He was more concerned about a thick-bellied Buddha who sat upon a huge horse. This, Stuart knew, would be General Shimokado.

The general climbed stiffly down. "*Akai Tatsu*, the Red Dragon. Where is he?"

"*Achi!*" said Stuart, pointing up the incline. "There." He shook his head sorrowfully. "But I had to kill him, General. He would not allow himself to be taken alive. He shot and killed my soldiers, but I managed to kill him, finally."

"Ah. I had thought to reserve that pleasure for myself." The general wallowed up the incline, puffing. When he went into the pit he stared down at the body and smiled. "Thin, wasn't he?"

"We kept him on the run in China, General."

89

Shimokado laughed, and the sound was like the bellow of a bull. "And you have things in hand in China, Blakely? I have heard something of you in Jehol, you see. We have often wanted to meet the man who keeps us in complete touch with the foreigners and the Chinese fools."

Stuart bowed and sighed. The sigh was one of intense relief. With greater boldness, he said, "And I have other news for you. General Chang has mobilized across the Wall, and an attack would not be successful at this time.

"And something else," said Stuart. "This lady here—"

"Ah, yes," said Shimokado, bowing. "What of her?"

"She has been of great aid to me in capturing the Red Dragon. She made believe that she loved him, and thereby led him on."

"Clever," said Shimokado. "I shall see that she gets a reward."

"But," continued Stuart, "I still have other news. Your brother is dead. Has been for some months. I do not know all the facts, but I know that he died.

"And," said Stuart, "I have been found out in China. They know that I killed Sheldon and his expedition in order to get the chart, and they also know that I have been reporting to you. Now that I have killed the Red Dragon, for he had many friends, it would not be advisable for me to go back."

"Quite true," said Shimokado. "But you have served us well, and you have some little pay coming to you, besides the reward I have in my saddlebags. Do you want it now?"

"Now is as good as any other time," said Stuart, smiling.

The general issued orders for the "Red Dragon's" body to

be buried. He did not seem concerned about anything else. He wallowed down to the pass and the waiting horsemen, followed by Stuart and Betty Sheldon. Stuart carried the burlap bags.

"What of the treasure you mentioned?" asked the general.

"It is here." Stuart reached into a bag and brought out a handful of brown figures which were well carved but without luster.

The general took one and tossed it in his palm. He snorted. "Some cave man's idea of art!" he said. "Utterly worthless. Keep it."

Stuart bowed, proceeding to tie the bags together. While they waited for some of Blakely's horses to be brought up, General Shimokado, possessed now of an easy mind, patted Stuart's shoulder.

"I have my car near here, Blakely. Less than twelve miles, it is. We'll go straight to the railroad and put you on a train for Port Arthur. A boat is sailing from there tomorrow night for the United States. You're a rich man now, Blakely. Fifty thousand dollars in American money should last a long while."

Stuart nodded.

Two nights later, aboard a Canadian boat outward bound, a well-dressed gentleman stood beside a well-dressed lady at the rail and helped her watch the moon rise out of the east.

"It isn't so odd," said the former Red Dragon, who was now buried in Manchuria. "You can't expect a general to be very intelligent about anything but generaling. He didn't know as much about archaeology as that moon does. Those burlap sacks in there, which are so heavy, contain what is known as tomb jade."

"Tomb jade!" said Betty.

"Yes. Contact with a human body in the grave turns jade to an ugly brown. I was saving this for a surprise, because I didn't think you could stand anything else. So those little carved figures, when cleaned up, prove to be valuable beyond any collector's dream. It's a million-dollar wedding present I'm giving you, Betty Sheldon."

"Wedding present?"

"Certainly," said Stuart, looking at his watch. "I told the captain that it would be at eight o'clock, and it's eight o'clock now. He dusted off the ship's Bible and he's all ready."

Betty Sheldon took his arm and walked on tiptoe beside him. As they started to enter the passageway to the officers' quarters above, she stopped and looked back.

"Don't," said Stuart with mock gruffness. "You've never heard of Manchuria and you've never heard of a Red Dragon. You and I were born tonight. Come along. The captain's waiting."

Story Preview

Story Preview

NOW that you've just ventured through one of the captivating tales in the Stories from the Golden Age collection by L. Ron Hubbard, turn the page and enjoy a preview of *The Devil—With Wings*. Join Captain Gary Forsythe of the Royal Marines, who launches a one-man invasion against the Japanese in war-torn China.

The Devil—With Wings

F ROM Shanghai to Vladivostok, the sight of this black-garbed white man had, for three years, been occasion for various types of heart failure among the soldiers of the Rising Sun.

Of his face only his nostrils and mouth were visible. The black leather flying helmet and the huge goggles were more effective than any mask. The black artillery boots looked staunch and solid but he could walk like a panther in them.

There were only three spots of light about him: the lens of each goggle and the large silver buckle of his belt.

His lips curved downward into a chilly grin as he stepped noiselessly over the Japanese and slid silent as a thundercloud along the black passageway.

He turned a corner and came to a stop. The glazed glass of one door exuded a thin yellow light, diffused until it spread like a saffron fog through the gloom. The ideograph on the door said, "Records."

Forsythe reached toward the knob but an instant before he touched it, a shadow became sharply outlined on the other side. The cap and profile of a Japanese, the silhouette of a fixed bayonet.

Instead of touching the knob, Forsythe stepped closer and made a fist of his glove.

He knocked sharply and the sound of it went booming through the brooding structure like a war drum.

The silhouette straightened and turned. The knob rattled. Yellow light spread from top to bottom in a long, widening line. The sentry stood there with bayonet at ready, peering into the gloom.

He saw the tall black shadow before him, caught the terrifying glitter of the goggles. The sentry needed no time for decision. He lunged and light streaked down the cold steel.

Forsythe stepped nimbly aside. He knew bayonets.

The gloves gripped the barrel as the bayonet dashed past. With a wrench, Forsythe whipped the weapon out of the sentry's hands and delivered a vicious butt stroke to the jaw.

Forsythe placed the rifle against the wall and stepped over the Japanese and into the Records room.

An unshaded electric light was burning above a littered, scarred table. The walls were lined with the tarnished brass handles of the files.

Without hesitation he strode to a cabinet and jerked it open. The black gloves gathered up large handfuls of paper to throw them upward and back. The sheets rustled and settled like enormous snowflakes over the rug.

Forsythe located the file he required and chuckled softly as he read his name blazoned in large ideographs across the top of it: THE DEVIL WITH WINGS.

He stepped to the table and started to sit down. A sound

held him crouched for an instant and then he straightened up and paced to the window and studied the street below.

A chunky Japanese car had drawn up to the curb before the office and now three officers were getting out. They looked squat and bearish in their greatcoats under the hard light from the street lamp.

Looking down at their precise round hats, Forsythe tried to recognize them. They stood talking for several seconds and then the leanest one of the lot started toward the entrance of the building. He looked up just before he stepped inside.

Forsythe drew hastily back.

It was Shinohari of the Japanese Intelligence.

The other two officers stayed by the car.

Forsythe paced again to the table and ripped into the file he had found. He tossed papers to the right and left until he came upon a thick wad of posters. He crammed a number of these into his jacket and then raced his glance across a clip of letters, singling out a pair, one of which read:

Captain Ito Shinohari
Imperial Japanese Army Headquarters

Honorable Sir:
   The American engineer Robert Weston was murdered yesterday near Aigun on the Amur River. Evidence indicates that he was killed by The Devil With Wings, *Akuma-no-Hané.*

N-38 at Aigun
Decoded by Lt. Tatsu
April 2

The other said:

Captain Shinohari:
Enclosed herewith a letter from Robert Weston to one Patricia Weston, his sister, mentioning value of a Confucius image. Original letter forwarded to Patricia Weston. As image may contain some secret document, suggest you follow lead to Patricia Weston. The hand of *Akuma-no-Hané* is quite plain in this.

Colonel Shimizu
Commanding Aigun
April 6

He wadded these into a small packet and slipped them into the heavy money belt at his waist.

For a moment he stood listening, looking at the door. He knew that Shinohari would find the unconscious sentry at the top of the steps, but *Akuma-no-Hané* preferred to let events take their own course.

Again he shuffled through the papers, watching for any detail which might serve him well. He missed the copy of the original letter to Patricia Weston though he tried hard to find it.

Another communication came under his hand:

Captain Ito Shinohari
Imperial Japanese Army Intelligence
Port Arthur

Honorable Sir:
May this unworthy agent be allowed to report that, after two days of constant watching, Patricia Weston has not yet contacted *Akuma-no-Hané*. May this one humbly

request relief from his post, knowing he can better serve the gallant Captain in other departments better.

In information it has been learned that Patricia Weston is without funds and it is not likely that she will leave Port Arthur. As ordered, this one has carefully undermined her credit at her hotel and at the cable station. There is therefore no likelihood of her leaving, or communicating with any possible friends in the United States.

This one suggests that it might be prudent to cause her to be deported at government expense.

N-16 at Port Arthur
May 3

Akuma-no-Hané slid this with the others into his money belt. He slapped the file into chaos about the room and strode to the Records office door, .45 drawn.

Before he could reach the knob it slammed toward him!

Shinohari, Luger in hand, was framed in the opening. Three feet from him Forsythe had centered the muzzle of the .45 automatic upon the yellow greatcoat.

They stood there, deadlocked, glaring at each other.

To find out more about *The Devil—With Wings* and how you can obtain your copy, go to www.goldenagestories.com.

Glossary

Glossary

STORIES FROM THE GOLDEN AGE *reflect the words and expressions used in the 1930s and 1940s, adding unique flavor and authenticity to the tales. While a character's speech may often reflect regional origins, it also can convey attitudes common in the day. So that readers can better grasp such cultural and historical terms, uncommon words or expressions of the era, the following glossary has been provided.*

Aigun: a town in northern Manchuria, situated on the Amur River.

Akai Tatsu!: (Japanese) Red Dragon!

Amur River: the world's ninth longest river that forms the border between northeastern China (Manchuria) and the Russian Far East (between Siberia and the Pacific Ocean). It was an area of conflict during the war between China and Japan that began in 1937, and eventually led to World War II in the Pacific.

anvil chorus: in reference to a piece of music, "The Troubadour," by Italian composer Giuseppe Verdi (1813–1901), that depicts Spanish gypsies striking their anvils at dawn and singing the praises of hard work, good wine and their gypsy women.

Canton: city and port in the southern part of China, northwest of Hong Kong.

Cossacks: members of a people of southern European Russia and adjacent parts of Asia, noted as cavalrymen especially during tzarist times. The Cossacks, known for their horses and horsemanship, were considered to be unequaled anywhere on Earth. In 1892, a troupe of Cossack daredevil riders joined the Buffalo Bill's Wild West show, traveling to London and then to America in 1893. Intrigued by the Cossacks' trick riding and stunts on their galloping horses, the Western cowboys soon introduced variations to American rodeo.

Cossack saddle: a saddle design that consists of two crosstrees in tandem (the wooden pieces at the front and rear of the saddle that form the pommel or saddle horn and cantle), with a leather pillow buckled down between them. The strap across the pillow is the secret of a Cossack's ability to ride standing up. He hooks his toes through the belt and the possibility of falling off is slight.

crosstree: the raised wooden pieces at the front and rear of the saddle that form a high pommel or horn in the front and cantle in the back.

dragnet: a systematic and coordinated search for a wanted person.

embrasure: 1. an opening in a thick wall for a portal or window, especially one with angled sides, so that the opening is larger on the inside than the outside. From the Old French embraser for "to cut at a slant." 2. the low segment of the alternating high and low segments of a battlement along the outer top of a wall or tower, through which weapons may be fired.

Forbidden City: a walled enclosure of central Peking, China, containing the palaces of twenty-four emperors in the Ming (1364–1644) and Qing (1644–1911) dynasties. It was formerly closed to the public, hence its name.

General Chang: Chang Hsüeh-liang (1901–2001); nicknamed "Young Marshal," he became the military governor of Manchuria after the assassination of his father, a major warlord of China, by the Japanese in 1928. He was made vice commander in chief of all Chinese forces and a member of the central political council. He made historic contributions to ending the ten-year (1927–1937) civil war, helping realize the cooperation between the Nationalist regime and the Communist Party of China, and making the whole nation take part in the war of resistance against Japanese aggression.

G-men: government men; agents of the Federal Bureau of Investigation.

Gobi: Asia's largest desert, located in China and southern Mongolia.

Gulliver in Brobdingnag: refers to a satire, *Gulliver's Travels*, by Jonathan Swift, in 1726. Lemuel Gulliver, an Englishman, travels to exotic lands, including Lilliput (where the people are six inches tall), Brobdingnag (where the people are seventy feet tall), and the land of the Houyhnhnms (where horses are the intelligent beings, and humans, called Yahoos, are mute brutes of labor).

Harbin: the capital and largest city of Heilongjiang Province, in northeastern China.

heliograph: a device for signaling by means of a movable mirror that reflects beams of light, especially sunlight, to a distance.

high binders: killers belonging to secret criminal organizations that controlled the gambling and slave-girl rackets. The origin of the term "high binders" is generally conceded to lie in the assassin's custom of binding his hair tightly around the top of his head, under his hat, so that the police could not catch him by the pigtail.

Hotel du Pekin: in the 1930s it was considered one of the finest hotels in the Orient. Built in 1917, the hotel had 200 rooms with baths, a tea hall with nightly dancing and its own orchestra for classical dinner music. It also had a spacious roof garden overlooking the Forbidden City and the Legation Quarter (walled city within the city exclusively for foreigners).

ideograph: a graphic symbol that represents an idea, rather than a group of letters arranged according to a spoken language, as in Chinese or Japanese characters.

Inner Mongolia: an autonomous region of northeast China. Originally the southern section of Mongolia, it was annexed by China in 1635, later becoming an integral part of China in 1911.

Jehol: a former province in northeast China; traditionally the gateway to Mongolia, Jehol was the name used in the 1920s and 1930s for the Chinese province north of the Great Wall, west of Manchuria and east of Mongolia. It was seized by the Japanese in early 1933, and was annexed to Manchukuo and not restored to China until the end of World War II.

legation: the official headquarters of a diplomatic minister.

Legation Street: also known as the Legation Quarter; it was encircled by a wall and was a city within Peking exclusively for foreigners. It housed eleven foreign embassies and was off-limits to Chinese residents.

looie: lieutenant of the armed forces.

Luger: a German semiautomatic pistol introduced before World War I and named after German firearms expert George Luger (1849–1923).

Manchukuo: a former state of eastern Asia in Manchuria and eastern Inner Mongolia. In 1932 it was established as a puppet state (a country that is nominally independent, but in reality is under the control of another power) after the Japanese invaded Manchuria in 1931. It was returned to the Chinese government in 1945.

Manchuria: a region of northeast China comprising the modern-day provinces of Heilongjiang, Jilin and Liaoning. It was the homeland of the Manchu people, who conquered China in the seventeenth century, and was hotly contested by the Russians and the Japanese in the late nineteenth and early twentieth centuries. Chinese Communists gained control of the area in 1948.

Mex: Mexican peso; in 1732 it was introduced as a trade coin with China and was so popular that China became one of its principal consumers. Mexico minted and exported pesos to China until 1949. It was issued as both coins and paper money.

Mikado: the emperor of Japan; a title no longer used.

Morrison Street: street in Peking named after Australian

George Morrison (1862–1920), a journalist and political advisor to the Chinese government. The street was the center for commercial activities.

Nanking: city in eastern China, on the Yangtze River. Now called Nanjing, it is the capital of Jiangsu Province.

Nankou: a city located northeast of Peking, near the Great Wall.

Peking: now Beijing, China.

Percheron: a breed of powerful, rugged draft horses, originating in northern France, that are noted for their heavy muscles.

Port Arthur: a Chinese seaport surrounded by ocean on three sides. It was named after a British Royal Navy lieutenant who, during a war in 1860, towed his crippled ship into the harbor for repairs. The Russians and other Western powers then adopted the British name.

postern: a small gate or entrance.

Punch and Judy: characters of the Punch and Judy puppet show, a famous English comedy dating back to the seventeenth century, by way of France from Italy. It is performed using hand puppets in a tent-style puppet theater with a cloth backdrop and board in front. The puppeteer introduces the puppets from beneath the board so that they are essentially popping up to the stage area of the theater.

Pu Yi, Henry: (1906–1967) emperor of China (1908–1924) when he was expelled by revolution. In 1932, he was installed by the Japanese as the emperor of Manchukuo. At the end of World War II, he was imprisoned until

1959, when he was granted amnesty by the leader of the Communist government.

rest on his oars: to cease to make an effort.

Scheherazade: the female narrator of *The Arabian Nights*, who during one thousand and one adventurous nights saved her life by entertaining her husband, the king, with stories.

Shamo: Chinese name for the Gobi Desert; Asia's largest desert located in China and southern Mongolia.

Shanghai: city of eastern China at the mouth of the Yangtze River, and the largest city in the country. Shanghai was opened to foreign trade by treaty in 1842 and quickly prospered. France, Great Britain and the United States all held large concessions (rights to use land granted by a government) in the city until the early twentieth century.

swagger stick: a short metal-tipped cane.

taichō: (Japanese) leader of a small group.

Tartar: a member of any of the various tribes, chiefly Mongolian and Turkish, who, originally under the leadership of Genghis Khan, overran Asia and much of eastern Europe in the Middle Ages. Also a member of the descendants of these people.

Tientsin: seaport located southeast of Peking; China's third largest city and major transportation and trading center. Tientsin was a "Treaty Port," a generic term used to denote Chinese cities open to foreign residence and trade, usually the result of a treaty.

tsuwamono: (Japanese) soldier.

two bits: a quarter; during the colonial days, people used coins from all over the world. When the US adopted an official currency, the Spanish milled (machine-struck) dollar was chosen and it later became the model for American silver dollars. Milled dollars were easily cut apart into equal "bits" of eight pieces. Two bits would equal a quarter of a dollar.

USMC: United States Marine Corps.

Vladivostok: city and major port in southeastern Russia, on Golden Horn Bay, an inlet of the Sea of Japan. It is the last city on the eastern end of the Trans-Siberian Railway.

Western Hills: a range of hills in China, situated northwest of Peking, which contains structures from the Ming and Qing dynasties and has forests of pine and fir trees. The range is known for its many temples and has long been a religious retreat. It also serves as a retreat for Chinese scholars and members of the government and civil service.

wing collar: a shirt collar, used especially in men's formal clothing, in which the front edges are folded down in such a way as to resemble a pair of wings.

L. Ron Hubbard
in the Golden Age
of Pulp Fiction

In writing an adventure story
a writer has to know that he is adventuring
for a lot of people who cannot.
The writer has to take them here and there
about the globe and show them
excitement and love and realism.
As long as that writer is living the part of an
adventurer when he is hammering
the keys, he is succeeding with his story.

Adventuring is a state of mind.
If you adventure through life, you have a
good chance to be a success on paper.

Adventure doesn't mean globe-trotting,
exactly, and it doesn't mean great deeds.
Adventuring is like art.
You have to live it to make it real.

— *L. RON HUBBARD*

L. Ron Hubbard
and American
Pulp Fiction

Born March 13, 1911, L. Ron Hubbard lived a life at least as expansive as the stories with which he enthralled a hundred million readers through a fifty-year career.

Originally hailing from Tilden, Nebraska, he spent his formative years in a classically rugged Montana, replete with the cowpunchers, lawmen and desperadoes who would later people his Wild West adventures. And lest anyone imagine those adventures were drawn from vicarious experience, he was not only breaking broncs at a tender age, he was also among the few whites ever admitted into Blackfoot society as a bona fide blood brother. While if only to round out an otherwise rough and tumble youth, his mother was that rarity of her time—a thoroughly educated woman—who introduced her son to the classics of Occidental literature even before his seventh birthday.

But as any dedicated L. Ron Hubbard reader will attest, his world extended far beyond Montana. In point of fact, and as the son of a United States naval officer, by the age of eighteen he had traveled over a quarter of a million miles. Included therein were three Pacific crossings to a then still mysterious Asia, where he ran with the likes of Her British Majesty's agent-in-place

L. Ron Hubbard, left, at Congressional Airport, Washington, DC, 1931, with members of George Washington University flying club.

for North China, and the last in the line of Royal Magicians from the court of Kublai Khan. For the record, L. Ron Hubbard was also among the first Westerners to gain admittance to forbidden Tibetan monasteries below Manchuria, and his photographs of China's Great Wall long graced American geography texts.

Upon his return to the United States and a hasty completion of his interrupted high school education, the young Ron Hubbard entered George Washington University. There, as fans of his aerial adventures may have heard, he earned his wings as a pioneering barnstormer at the dawn of American aviation. He also earned a place in free-flight record books for the longest sustained flight above Chicago. Moreover, as a roving reporter for *Sportsman Pilot* (featuring his first professionally penned articles), he further helped inspire a generation of pilots who would take America to world airpower.

Immediately beyond his sophomore year, Ron embarked on the first of his famed ethnological expeditions, initially to then untrammeled Caribbean shores (descriptions of which would later fill a whole series of West Indies mystery-thrillers). That the Puerto Rican interior would also figure into the future of Ron Hubbard stories was likewise no accident. For in addition to cultural studies of the island, a 1932–33

LRH expedition is rightly remembered as conducting the first complete mineralogical survey of a Puerto Rico under United States jurisdiction.

There was many another adventure along this vein: As a lifetime member of the famed Explorers Club, L. Ron Hubbard charted North Pacific waters with the first shipboard radio direction finder, and so pioneered a long-range navigation system universally employed until the late twentieth century. While not to put too fine an edge on it, he also held a rare Master Mariner's license to pilot any vessel, of any tonnage in any ocean.

Yet lest we stray too far afield, there is an LRH note at this juncture in his saga, and it reads in part:

"I started out writing for the pulps, writing the best I knew, writing for every mag on the stands, slanting as well as I could."

To which one might add: His earliest submissions date from the summer of 1934, and included tales drawn from true-to-life Asian adventures, with characters roughly modeled on British/American intelligence operatives he had known in Shanghai. His early Westerns were similarly peppered with details drawn from personal

Capt. L. Ron Hubbard in Ketchikan, Alaska, 1940, on his Alaskan Radio Experimental Expedition, the first of three voyages conducted under the Explorers Club flag.

experience. Although therein lay a first hard lesson from the often cruel world of the pulps. His first Westerns were soundly rejected as lacking the authenticity of a Max Brand yarn

117

(a particularly frustrating comment given L. Ron Hubbard's Westerns came straight from his Montana homeland, while Max Brand was a mediocre New York poet named Frederick Schiller Faust, who turned out implausible six-shooter tales from the terrace of an Italian villa).

Nevertheless, and needless to say, L. Ron Hubbard persevered and soon earned a reputation as among the most publishable names in pulp fiction, with a ninety percent placement rate of first-draft manuscripts. He was also among the most prolific, averaging between seventy and a hundred thousand words a month. Hence the rumors that L. Ron Hubbard had redesigned a typewriter for faster keyboard action and pounded out manuscripts on a continuous roll of butcher paper to save the precious seconds it took to insert a single sheet of paper into manual typewriters of the day.

That all L. Ron Hubbard stories did not run beneath said byline is yet another aspect of pulp fiction lore. That is, as publishers periodically rejected manuscripts from top-drawer authors if only to avoid paying top dollar, L. Ron Hubbard and company just as frequently replied with submissions under various pseudonyms. In Ron's case, the list

A MAN OF MANY NAMES

Between 1934 and 1950, L. Ron Hubbard authored more than fifteen million words of fiction in more than two hundred classic publications. To supply his fans and editors with stories across an array of genres and pulp titles, he adopted fifteen pseudonyms in addition to his already renowned L. Ron Hubbard byline.

*Winchester Remington Colt
Lt. Jonathan Daly
Capt. Charles Gordon
Capt. L. Ron Hubbard
Bernard Hubbel
Michael Keith
Rene Lafayette
Legionnaire 148
Legionnaire 14830
Ken Martin
Scott Morgan
Lt. Scott Morgan
Kurt von Rachen
Barry Randolph
Capt. Humbert Reynolds*

118

included: Rene Lafayette, Captain Charles Gordon, Lt. Scott Morgan and the notorious Kurt von Rachen—supposedly on the lam for a murder rap, while hammering out two-fisted prose in Argentina. The point: While L. Ron Hubbard as Ken Martin spun stories of Southeast Asian intrigue, LRH as Barry Randolph authored tales of

L. Ron Hubbard, circa 1930, at the outset of a literary career that would finally span half a century.

romance on the Western range—which, stretching between a dozen genres is how he came to stand among the two hundred elite authors providing close to a million tales through the glory days of American Pulp Fiction.

In evidence of exactly that, by 1936 L. Ron Hubbard was literally leading pulp fiction's elite as president of New York's American Fiction Guild. Members included a veritable pulp hall of fame: Lester "Doc Savage" Dent, Walter "The Shadow" Gibson, and the legendary Dashiell Hammett—to cite but a few.

Also in evidence of just where L. Ron Hubbard stood within his first two years on the American pulp circuit: By the spring of 1937, he was ensconced in Hollywood, adopting a Caribbean thriller for Columbia Pictures, remembered today as *The Secret of Treasure Island.* Comprising fifteen thirty-minute episodes, the L. Ron Hubbard screenplay led to the most profitable matinée serial in Hollywood history. In accord with Hollywood culture, he was thereafter continually called

The 1937 Secret of Treasure Island, *a fifteen-episode serial adapted for the screen by L. Ron Hubbard from his novel,* Murder at Pirate Castle.

upon to rewrite/doctor scripts—most famously for long-time friend and fellow adventurer Clark Gable.

In the interim—and herein lies another distinctive chapter of the L. Ron Hubbard story—he continually worked to open Pulp Kingdom gates to up-and-coming authors. Or, for that matter, anyone who wished to write. It was a fairly unconventional stance, as markets were already thin and competition razor sharp. But the fact remains, it was an L. Ron Hubbard hallmark that he vehemently lobbied on behalf of young authors—regularly supplying instructional articles to trade journals, guest-lecturing to short story classes at George Washington University and Harvard, and even founding his own creative writing competition. It was established in 1940, dubbed the Golden Pen, and guaranteed winners both New York representation and publication in *Argosy*.

But it was John W. Campbell Jr.'s *Astounding Science Fiction* that finally proved the most memorable LRH vehicle. While every fan of L. Ron Hubbard's galactic epics undoubtedly knows the story, it nonetheless bears repeating: By late 1938, the pulp publishing magnate of Street & Smith was determined to revamp *Astounding Science Fiction* for broader readership. In particular, senior editorial director F. Orlin Tremaine called for stories with a stronger *human element*. When acting editor John W. Campbell balked, preferring his spaceship-driven tales,

Tremaine enlisted Hubbard. Hubbard, in turn, replied with the genre's first truly *character-driven* works, wherein heroes are pitted not against bug-eyed monsters but the mystery and majesty of deep space itself—and thus was launched the Golden Age of Science Fiction.

The names alone are enough to quicken the pulse of any science fiction aficionado, including LRH friend and protégé, Robert Heinlein, Isaac Asimov, A. E. van Vogt and Ray Bradbury. Moreover, when coupled with LRH stories of fantasy, we further come to what's rightly been described as the foundation of every modern tale of horror: L. Ron Hubbard's immortal *Fear*. It was rightly proclaimed by Stephen King as one of the very few works to genuinely warrant that overworked term "classic"—as in: *"This is a classic tale of creeping, surreal menace and horror. . . . This is one of the really, really good ones."*

L. Ron Hubbard, 1948, among fellow science fiction luminaries at the World Science Fiction Convention in Toronto.

To accommodate the greater body of L. Ron Hubbard fantasies, Street & Smith inaugurated *Unknown*—a classic pulp if there ever was one, and wherein readers were soon thrilling to the likes of *Typewriter in the Sky* and *Slaves of Sleep* of which Frederik Pohl would declare: *"There are bits and pieces from Ron's work that became part of the language in ways that very few other writers managed."*

And, indeed, at J. W. Campbell Jr.'s insistence, Ron was regularly drawing on themes from the Arabian Nights and

121

so introducing readers to a world of genies, jinn, Aladdin and Sinbad—all of which, of course, continue to float through cultural mythology to this day.

At least as influential in terms of post-apocalypse stories was L. Ron Hubbard's 1940 *Final Blackout*. Generally acclaimed as the finest anti-war novel of the decade and among the ten best works of the genre ever authored—here, too, was a tale that would live on in ways few other writers

Portland,
Oregon, 1943;
L. Ron Hubbard
captain of the
US Navy subchaser
PC 815.

imagined. Hence, the later Robert Heinlein verdict: "Final Blackout *is as perfect a piece of science fiction as has ever been written.*"

Like many another who both lived and wrote American pulp adventure, the war proved a tragic end to Ron's sojourn in the pulps. He served with distinction in four theaters and was highly decorated for commanding corvettes in the North Pacific. He was also grievously wounded in combat, lost many a close friend and colleague and thus resolved to say farewell to pulp fiction and devote himself to what it had supported these many years—namely, his serious research.

But in no way was the LRH literary saga at an end, for as he wrote some thirty years later, in 1980:

"Recently there came a period when I had little to do. This was novel in a life so crammed with busy years, and I decided to amuse myself by writing a novel that was pure science fiction."

That work was *Battlefield Earth: A Saga of the Year 3000*. It was an immediate *New York Times* bestseller and, in fact, the first international science fiction blockbuster in decades. It was not, however, L. Ron Hubbard's magnum opus, as that distinction is generally reserved for his next and final work: The 1.2 million word *Mission Earth*.

> **Final Blackout**
> *is as perfect a piece of science fiction as has ever been written.*
>
> —Robert Heinlein

How he managed those 1.2 million words in just over twelve months is yet another piece of the L. Ron Hubbard legend. But the fact remains, he did indeed author a ten-volume *dekalogy* that lives in publishing history for the fact that each and every volume of the series was also a *New York Times* bestseller.

Moreover, as subsequent generations discovered L. Ron Hubbard through republished works and novelizations of his screenplays, the mere fact of his name on a cover signaled an international bestseller. . . . Until, to date, sales of his works exceed hundreds of millions, and he otherwise remains among the most enduring and widely read authors in literary history. Although as a final word on the tales of L. Ron Hubbard, perhaps it's enough to simply reiterate what editors told readers in the glory days of American Pulp Fiction:

He writes the way he does, brothers, because he's been there, seen it and done it!

THE STORIES FROM THE GOLDEN AGE

Your ticket to adventure starts here with the Stories from
the Golden Age collection by master storyteller L. Ron Hubbard.
These gripping tales are set in a kaleidoscope of exotic locales and brim
with fascinating characters, including some of the
most vile villains, dangerous dames and brazen heroes
you'll ever get to meet.

The entire collection of over one hundred and fifty stories is being
released in a series of eighty books and audiobooks.
For an up-to-date listing of available titles,
go to www.goldenagestories.com.

AIR ADVENTURE

Arctic Wings   *Man-Killers of the Air*
The Battling Pilot   *On Blazing Wings*
Boomerang Bomber   *Red Death Over China*
The Crate Killer   *Sabotage in the Sky*
The Dive Bomber   *Sky Birds Dare!*
Forbidden Gold   *The Sky-Crasher*
Hurtling Wings   *Trouble on His Wings*
The Lieutenant Takes the Sky *Wings Over Ethiopia*

FAR-FLUNG ADVENTURE

SEA ADVENTURE

TALES FROM THE ORIENT

The Devil—With Wings   *Pearl Pirate*
The Falcon Killer   *The Red Dragon*
Five Mex for a Million   *Spy Killer*
Golden Hell   *Tah*
The Green God   *The Trail of the Red Diamonds*
Hurricane's Roar   *Wind-Gone-Mad*
Inky Odds   *Yellow Loot*
Orders Is Orders

MYSTERY

The Blow Torch Murder   *The Grease Spot*
Brass Keys to Murder   *Killer Ape*
Calling Squad Cars!   *Killer's Law*
The Carnival of Death   *The Mad Dog Murder*
The Chee-Chalker   *Mouthpiece*
Dead Men Kill   *Murder Afloat*
The Death Flyer   *The Slickers*
Flame City   *They Killed Him Dead*

127

FANTASY

SCIENCE FICTION

WESTERN

129

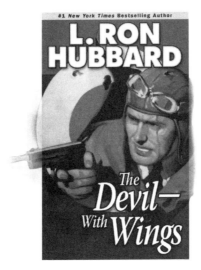

JOIN THE PULP REVIVAL
America in the 1930s and 40s

Pulp fiction was in its heyday and 30 million readers were regularly riveted by the larger-than-life tales of master storyteller L. Ron Hubbard. For this was pulp fiction's golden age, when the writing was raw and every page packed a walloping punch.

That magic can now be yours. An evocative world of nefarious villains, exotic intrigues, courageous heroes and heroines—a world that today's cinema has barely tapped for tales of adventure and swashbucklers.

Enroll today in the Stories from the Golden Age Club and begin receiving your monthly feature edition selected from more than 150 stories in the collection.

You may choose to enjoy them as either a paperback or audiobook for the special membership price of $9.95 each month along with FREE shipping and handling.